Mythical Desire

Arian Mabe

This collection of short, erotic tales is inspired by Welsh myths and legends.

This collection contains a mix of sexual pairings and characters in various romantic and new relationships with one another.

The stories in this collection contain: cisgender anthros, transgender anthros, straight sex, gay sex, lesbian sex, oral sex, vaginal sex, anal sex, masturbation, a threesome, sex toys, light domination and submission play, sex outdoors and risking getting caught.

Cover art by Alena Bodrova.

Table of Contents

Dragons and Their Mead

The tavern nestled into the Welsh hills bustled with activity, though one would not have called it a hive, even with the jovial hum in the air. There were too many creatures in there, though so very few of the insectoid variety, to consider it such, with magically powered lights hanging from the ceiling, flickering with the mimicked glow of candlelight. The old oak and pine furniture had seen better days, some chairs with notches taken out of them, but weapon use in the tavern had been banned long ago; that didn't stop some wayward adventurers from dragging in swords and maces anyway. It was hard to keep an eye on everyone at once while the staff hustled plates of steaming food out to tables and the barkeep kept the drinks flowing freely.

Wolves sat with cats and distrustful badgers eyed the scurrying voles with a curious eye, keeping guard over their territory – even though they couldn't really call Halfway Tavern a territory at all. Yet those regulars that the barkeep knew would say it was their place, their spot and their right, defending it vehemently.

Especially from outsiders, of course. And who could be considered more of an outsider than a white dragon? The drake sat back in his chair, a leg kicked out, a flagon of ale in his clawed hand. There were few pale-scaled dragons to be found there and it was clear from anyone who spoke to him that his accent was not of the mountains and valleys of Wales.

On the round table before him, which the dragon did not share, lay an open scroll, a quill in a pot of ink beside it. Although a few words had been scratched in moderately passable script on the scroll itself, it did not appear the dragon had made all that much progress with what he was writing, though many curious looks came his way. With two elegant horns and a fine line of spines running down his back that seemed to flatten to his spine, there was a sense of refinement about him that did not fit at all with the usual clientele of Halfway Tavern.

The white drake drew attention, however, and a chestnut stallion smirked and buried his nose in his tankard as a less polished sort moved past him. For where there was a white dragon from England visiting their way, on his travels, there would most usually be found a red dragon from Wales to match up to him. It was the way of it: one of those funny happenings that no one thought to question all that much, or perhaps it was the saying perpetuating itself into truth indefinitely.

Bigger and bulkier than the white dragon's narrower frame, Sirous approached with a languid roll to his gate, somehow seamlessly sliding between tables that had been placed too close together. For his muscled heft, he did not at all look as if he should have moved with that grace, yet Sirous did so all the same, his large horns weighty and curved like those of a ram, dominating his face. The curve of his cheek had a sharper line to it, meeting his jaw, than the English drake's did and his scales seemed somewhat rougher around the edges. If he had been hewn from stone, the white drake's body had been moulded by water, the edges of his frame softened and smoothed.

As Sirous stopped at his table, his hand resting casually on the hilt of his sword, the white dragon finally glanced up at him. There was an ink spot on his right hand that he didn't seem to have noticed, standing out starkly against the otherwise gleaming, white scales there. The difference between them was more comical than ever with Sirous so near, the red of his scales almost rude to the eye, but the white drake's attire was more elegant in a tunic, flowing trousers and finely made leather boots than Sirous'. It was hardly the sort of thing Sirous would have noted, but the dirt on his boots and the worn hem of his cloak betrayed a life led more simply, replacing what he wore only when he needed it. However, he was dressed casually enough for an evening meal and a drink at the tavern, with a tunic and more practical trousers under his cloak.

"And what may I do for you?" The white dragon said, his lips pressing together and a glint in his eye as he was forced to look up at Sirous. "Do dragons attract dragons here?"

Sirous hid his smirk, though his wings shuffled under his cloak, where they were folded in neatly against his back.

"You, sir, are barely alike me, beyond being a dragon," Sirous drawled, lips twitching in faint amusement. "But I haven't seen you at Halfway Tavern before. Perhaps you are *halfway* somewhere else?"

The dragon eyed him as if Sirous was imposing, yet he did not make a move to leave and neither did he sent Sirous away.

"Well, dear sir, I am a poet," he drawled, casting the red drake a less than appraising look up and down. "I wouldn't think you'd know any of that, however…"

The red dragon raised the ridge of an eyebrow, the tip of his tail twitching. Yet his expression otherwise remained plain, despite his inner amusement at an English drake's folly.

"Oh, you could try me," he said, drawing out a chair with a scrape of wood on the old, stone floor, though it barely drew a look from anyone near. "I read some, of course. There has to be something to do by firelight when camping between towns. By the way, I don't seem to have your name."

The white dragon snorted mildly and sat up a little, his hands folded together on the table before him.

"George," he said shortly. "A good, English name."

Sirous' eyes gleamed.

"And mine is a good, Welsh name. So, we have found one way in which we are counterparts."

The poet, George, grunted under his breath, but the drake did not deign to comment on that one. He could answer or he could ignore what Sirous had to say, but his tail curled back and forth under the table, undulating faintly. It may have been out of sight of Sirous, but the connection between them still crackled through the air, like the hum of electricity after a lightning strike.

Sirous' breath hitched, ever so slightly. George didn't notice as he adjusted the V-neck of his tunic, where it plunged between his pectoral muscles. His chest was narrower than Sirous' and still the dragon's eyes dropped to the exposed scales, a gleam of hunger in his eyes.

"So, why are you here, Poet George?" Sirous probed, accepting a flagon of his usual mead from the barkeep who sent a fox server over to keep them both hydrated. "This is hardly a place for a dragon like you…and you do not appear all that thrilled to be here either?"

George swallowed and poked a finger suspiciously at his own flagon of mead, which had been set on the table before him.

"What is this?"

"Ah, are you just trying to avoid the question?"

George scowled and Sirous shot him a sly grin.

"Not at all," he said stiffly, wings shuffling against the back of his chair. "I was merely wondering what I had been handed here."

Sirous nodded at the drake's empty wine glass, though it was not something kept stocked all that often at taverns like Halfway. The clientele did not tend to be refined, but Aled must have had a few bottles from the vineyard in stock. It wasn't bad, though Sirous preferred the imported bottles when they came by, or what had been aged, drawn up from dusty cellars. It was truly amazing what bonuses came his way while adventuring, whether he was ridding an estate of a spider-morph infestation or taking care of a horde of those flying serpents, slithering into dwellings where they did not belong. Many were grateful for his services, though delving deep into the mountains and caverns as yet unexplored would always be Sirous' true passion in life.

"It's mead," he said with a shuffling of his wings, unclasping his cloak and slinging it casually over the back of his chair in one fluid motion. "Have you not enjoyed it before?"

George pressed his lips together, the line of them tightening mildly.

"Indeed. But I did not enjoy."

"I imagine there is very little you enjoy, but I'm confident we can find maybe one or two things here that take your fancy, sir," Sirous said with a grin. "Drink. It's on me. If you'll tell your story as to why you're here, how you are travelling…"

George sighed. In a way, his poetry writing, in public as he was, drew attention he wanted for himself – but a brutish drake was hardly the kind of attention he wanted. He wanted to be held aloft, to have his works held in high regard. He wanted others to look at him with admiration in their eyes, in awe of his words.

Only…he had not quite reached that level of acclaim, not yet. In fact, George was far from it. But he wasn't going to let that on to Sirous.

"If it shall make you be quiet…"

He took a sip from the mead and found it sweeter than he remembered, though the honey would do such to it, he was sure. That could be a good note for his poems and he scratched away absently at the scroll, adding a few more notes. That scroll had turned merely into one for notes and even George's latest poems would take a greater amount of refinement.

Sirous stared expectantly at him, elbows on the table and the flagon at his lips. George sighed, minutely.

"I have come from London to see your…quaint country," he said, though his shoulders eased as he spoke. "It really is quite beautiful, for we do not have the variance in terrain where I grew up. The flat plains, however, stretch all the way down to the ocean, far on the East coast… I've written about those."

"Ah, Llundain," Sirous said with a nod. "I rarely travel that far, not all the way to the city, but my forays take me into Lloegr from time to time. Not far over the border these days."

George blinked, taking a moment to catch up with Sirous' casual use of language.

"Ah… Lloegr," he repeated, mimicking Sirous' manner of speaking without thinking about it. "I saw that on the sign as I came over. That's your word for England, correct? You speak English well."

"A word is a word," Sirous said with a shrug and a swallow of mead. "But that doesn't change what something is, the meaning of the thing itself."

George's brow furrowed.

"That makes no sense in the slightest."

"It does if you think hard enough about it."

George grunted and drank to cover up the quiet – and to save him from finding words quickly to fill that quiet. He was better when he got to think a little more about what he was saying, taking his time. Sometimes, moments rushed by, however, and left him behind.

"Regardless, I am travelling to broaden my view of the world, a tour of sorts," George went on. "I'm afraid there is little more to it than that. There is only so much cavorting around playhouses with males buying me fine wines one can abide before they need to strike out."

Sirous let out a bark of laughter.

"Oh, is that your life then?" He teased, as if he and George were older friends than they were – and they were barely acquaintances. "Enjoying the busy life in *London*, the hype and the bustle? Why would you give all that up to travel out here?"

George tilted his head, taking in the other dragon's visage once again. His eyes lingered on the almost mane-like protrusion of softer spines at the back of Sirous' head. They curled "up" from the back of his head like the crest of a bird and, already, George felt himself to be more inspired in the other drake's presence than he had been in months."

"I have already said," George grumbled, less than patiently. "I am writing poetry, seeing the country."

"Yes, but many take magical transport, perhaps gryphon riding or similar, to visit the countries over the sea," Sirous said with a smile. "Why here? You seem conflicted on what our mountains have to offer you."

George paused, drinking more of his mead. It was soothing, slipping down his throat, as he swallowed hard, a dribble of it marking the corner of his lips. His tail twitched and, less than surreptitiously, he drank more, filling the space between them. In a way, it was comforting.

"There is much beauty to be had here, but I fear I might not be the one to uncover it," he said slowly, taking his time with his words. "Though I hardly know why I'm telling you this. Perhaps it is as you are a stranger to me. If you knew me, I would have more to say that I do not mean."

Sirous surveyed him.

"It is a shame not to be open with those you know better," he said, gesturing to the barkeep to send them more mead, for theirs was disappearing at quite a pace. "But I would like to know you better, George, and I've hardly known you for any time at all."

George gave him a look that could have meant anything. Sirous smiled as the flagons landed on the table again, the waiter swiftly collecting their used ones so they could be washed back in the kitchen.

"Thanks, David," he said quietly to the younger wolf who'd come out with the drinks. "And you… I hope you find what you want here, though you may find yourself staying longer than expected."

George leaned forward, his tongue feeling oddly loose with the mead he'd consumed. Maybe that was why he was talking more than normal – yet more naturally than usual too. What did he have to lose by speaking freely, after all? Gone was the mask he wore, putting it on so those in London and the surrounding, sprawling towns would see him as one of their own. Yet he was not even sure, not yet, where he belonged.

"Oh, I think your sleepy Welsh towns would bore me in time," he said with a hint of a tease in his tone, softening somewhat. "I think they would tire of me too. Look at how you've approached me."

"I've approached you while others did not and sitting with a stranger is not something I am all that accustomed to either," Sirous confessed with a smile. "I am more of a solitary sort."

George snorted into his mead.

"No, you don't say?"

"What gave it away?"

The dragons laughed lightly, another layer of strangeness between them stripped away. The honey mead warmed them through and the tavern fell away, as if they were the only two anthros left in the world, tails curling and uncurling slowly under the table. They did not go unnoticed, but the barkeep kept an eye out for them, the old fox's muzzle greying faintly. Yet he scanned the bar even as he dried a flagon swiftly, his staff running back and forth with food and drinks, though it was the latter that flowed more freely as the hour grew late.

Yet the dragons did not leave. They leaned in closer and closer to one another with every subsequent flagon of mead, chairs scooting closer until their arms brushed one another. They might have been hard-pressed to recount what they had talked about, come the next day, but they would remember the details as if they had already been a part of their lives together.

Like the school George had gone to and the headmaster who strode through the halls with a black cloak flapping around his legs.

And the story of the first sword Sirous had ever wielded, too large for him at a younger age and dragging on the ground where he struggled to lift it.

The moment of George accidentally letting his tail lay against Sirous' under the table – then forgetting to lift it away again.

And the tale of the latest adventure Sirous had gone on, which had George hanging off his every word, imagining the fight recounted in his mind's eye, Sirous' muscles bunching and releasing with every strike.

And then there was Sirous resting his wing against George's back, inviting the dragon in against the side of his body, an arm going around the white-scaled dragon when the moment felt right. They fit together as if their forms had been designed especially for one another, but life wasn't about all those light, gentle moments where everything went perfectly. It would have been tiresome, truly, if so, for the sharp edges and bumps were what made the reality of life, especially with another.

Eventually, however, the tavern grew darker, the barkeep giving Sirous a knowing nod that the dragon had to abide by. Most of the stragglers were returning to their homes or heading to the stairs of the tavern where accommodations were on the next floor up, though the dragon had not asked his new companion where he was staying yet.

"I think it is our time to close the night, George," Sirous said slowly, curling his wing back to his back and noticing just how George leaned in closer to him. "Where are you staying? I can walk you back."

"Oh…"

George looked down, fumbling with his scroll, which had been set aside in lieu of their conversation.

"I see, I understand," he said, striving and failing to hide the undercurrent of disappointment thrumming through him; mead would do that to a dragon, as good as it felt swilling through his system. "I am actually staying just upstairs here, for a few days…"

"Then…may I return to your room with you?"

He didn't want to be too forward about things – but he hadn't come to his place in life from holding back. He couldn't hold back from the strike when he was out adventuring and he couldn't still his arm when he wanted to slide it around the narrow curve of George's waist. It seemed only natural for his hand to rest on the dragon's hip, folding around where the bone rose close to the skin, the slender dragon boasting a figure Sirous would love to have under him.

There was only one answer George wanted to give, despite the heat rising to his cheeks and crawling temptingly down his neck. He nodded and allowed Sirous to guide him up from his seat, leaning more heavily on to him than he really had to for support. It was just another excuse for him to be close to Sirous, revelling in that scale-to-scale contact as much as he could greedily drink in the sensation. It was only a good thing, at least in his mind, that his scales hid the heat on his face, as did fur on many other anthros in the world. Humans, or any folk with skin rather than anything to cover it, didn't have that luxury.

Sirous grinned, heart hammering, as he followed George up the narrow, creaky staircase, though he hoped the bed in George's room was not quite as noisy. The white dragon only fumbled for a moment with the key he'd been given in the lock of his room, the door number marked in carved, wooden numbers in the centre.

The room itself, as they thumped inside with expectation curling around them, was simply furnished with a single, small wardrobe and a bed that would have been a very tight fit for two to sleep on it. The room itself was large enough for the dragons to move around the outside of the bed and look out the window without being too cramped, but it would not have held all that much furniture, if the owner of the tavern thought to ever add any more. Maybe there were rooms there with wider, double beds intended for two bodies to warm one another at night, but Sirous doubted it. The tavern was not a large establishment and it looked like the rooms upstairs were originally intended for the owner to sleep in, some time ago. Lives changed, however, and they had likely needed more space as their family had grown.

"George…"

He couldn't resist saying the dragon's name out loud, even though George did not yet understand how similar they were, their names variations of the same. But the sound of that name on his lips simply felt right, even if part of that was purely his proximity to the dragon, still enjoying how his tongue curled and wrapped around the name in his mouth.

Still, he had to set it free, sooner or later, and George folded into Sirous with heat in his cheeks. Sirous grinned and ran his thumb along the side of George's muzzle, the fingers of his right hand curled under his narrow, delicate jaw as that very thumb teased up to his cheek.

"You're blushing," he murmured, a little shiver running through him. "I can feel it. I love it."

George trembled, tipping his head back. When the dragons were standing, it was more obvious that Sirous was taller than George's slight frame, the white drake needing to tip his head back as Sirous' fingers trailed down, the tips of his claws grazing George's throat.

He moaned, lips parting.

"Oh…"

As soon as his lips parted for that utterance, a cry that begged so much more, Sirous' lips were on his, hungrily kissing, tempting with an open-mouthed embrace. George whimpered into it and then their hands were on one other, grasping and pulling at clothing, striving to hastily strip on another with mead and lust flowing through their bodies.

Their lips moved wantonly against one another, Sirous tossing his cloak to the side, though the dragon didn't much care where it landed. Not as his tongue snaked into George's maw and swept against his own tongue, coaxing the other drake into kissing him more deeply, giving in to those deeper, primal urges.

It was not the mead, though the drink sometimes could be a facilitator to such connection, erotic tension thrumming between them as George groaned into Sirous' mouth. His head swirled pleasantly, like his body was humming with need, but there was no doubt at all in the white-scaled drake's mind he was going to get what he needed from that moment, longing to give all he could to Sirous too.

Sirous hissed as George's hands managed to get his tunic up and over his head, glad at least that he'd dressed more casually that day. His sword was the more awkward thing with its weight at his hip in the scabbard, but Sirous took care of that as he unfastened it at his hip, letting the belt that held it in place slide to the ground. It had been loose, anyway, for he rarely kept it on when not out in the mountains, on a quest. The only reason Sirous had the sword with him in the tavern had been because he'd had a repair done to the handle with the town blacksmith.

With his torso bare and the annoying scrape of the leather scabbard gone from where it had lain directly against his scales with the tunic gone, he grasped the drake passionately and drew George with him as he fell back on the bed. They kissed, legs scrabbling together to find a place for every limb, though their tails instinctively wanted to tangle, fighting to curl around one another. That tease of possessiveness was something many drakes fought with: a hangover from greedier days long gone by where they would have a hoard and collect all that sang to their hearts. Still, their want to keep a partner all to themselves rendered them, at the bare minimum, monogamous.

But neither dragon was thinking about that in the slightest as they kissed and fought with their trousers, Sirous' sliding down more easily as his undergarments came along with his clothes. He groaned as his hardness rose, the tip of his shaft having been pushing out from the slit at the base. Without that restriction, it slipped free and rose to attention, a thick, throbbing length of dragon-shaft begging attention as a poet's trembling fingers eased along it.

"Ah… You're large."

George shivered, a ripple running down his body. It cumulated in the tip of his tail, which wiggled faintly, though the dragons were so close Sirous didn't notice it. His heart skipped a beat, then appeared to beat harder in his chest – or maybe he was simply more in tune with his body, better able to feel the thrumming pulse of it after briefly grazing Sirous' cock with his fingertips.

Could he take something like that? But he didn't have to either, for there was one thing George was certain of between them and that there were no expectations. They might have any kind of sex there that night, but there was no chance either dragon would ever be in a position where they felt like they were being forced to perform in any way. It was all about the moment, the connection, and it didn't have to hold any more weight to it than that.

That was what had him relaxing against Sirous as the red dragon slowly worked down his trousers, freeing George's rising shaft that had been tenting out the front of them. Unlike Sirous, his shaft came with a starkly defined head with a rounded yet tapered tip – and a set of balls. Not all dragons were alike, after all, and sometimes they had a version of a slit, a cloaca or even external shafts and balls like George. Some dragons even had multiple cocks: now that would have been a challenge for George.

Sirous murmured as he stripped them both naked, kissing the dragon's thighs as he revealed him, licking his lips.

"Oh, you look good enough to devour," he growled, breath washing tentatively over George's cock as it throbbed, an unformed knot at the base and the length perfectly smooth, unlike his own lightly ridged member. "Please… May I?"

It took George a moment to realise Sirous was talking about his shaft, touching him – and he rushed to nod.

"Oh – yes, yes…"

Sirous chuckled softly, the sound layering under his breath, but didn't rush as he nuzzled in slowly, George on his back on the bed with his head up on the pillows. Although the pillows were, more often than not, reinforced to deal with the horns of anthros like them, the tips of his fine horns still dug into them, indenting the soft surface. If they tore, they'd have to talk to the tavern owner about replacing them, but that wasn't something they had to worry about.

George most certainly was not worrying about it as Sirous' lips ghosted over his hard member, lips pursing around the head of his shaft as his hand folded sensually around the girth. He moaned openly, rolling his hips up against Sirous, but the drake held him in good stead. Sirous let his tongue drape down against George's cock, sliding it around and testing just how much of the length of it he could wrap around the dragon's shaft. In fact, it was a surprising amount of it, the slippery appendage curling and dragging as George's breath hitched in his chest.

"Ah… Ohhh…"

He could barely get anything comprehensible out of his mouth as Sirous teased him, closing his maw around that sensitive rod of flesh. Oh, it was a delight to manage, to press his lips around the girth and feel the flesh of him growing slicker under his touch. His tongue was not of a good size to cradle a cock like that, but there was so much more Sirous could do with his lengthy tongue, slurping a little as he bobbed his head.

His fingers teased and fluttered around that girth, though the dragon should well enough have known that he was a good size too, their shafts rather closely matched. Sirous got the impression, however, that George was more used to being on the bottom.

He met the position well, moaning and coming sweetly apart as Sirous moaned around his cock, wanting to coax out every little sound and shudder from George. The white drake's tail tightened its grip on Sirous' red-scaled one and he leaned hungrily into that embrace, the blanket on the bed twisted and rumpled under George's body. Yet neither dragon cared to fix it when their forms fit so well against one another, George arching passionately up against Sirous, the frantic beat of his heart practically leaping out against his narrow chest.

George's head spun as Sirous lapped around him, sliding up to suck on the head of his shaft and closing his lips just behind the glands. He bucked against Sirous without thinking about what he was doing, as if Sirous had become all that mattered in the world, bringing him to a throbbing, whimpering crescendo with seemingly no effort at all.

Sirous' hands were far from idle in the moment too, sweeping over the dragon's thighs and playing back up over his hips and wandering over his abdominal muscles. They were smaller than his and tighter, but George reached for him too, fingers easing around the sensitive scales at the base of his horns. The dragon shuddered bodily, his own cock throbbing with anticipated delight in all that was to come.

He sucked on the drake's shaft, bobbing his head, but those hands quivered, fluttering away from his head a moment later and then brushing back against his cheeks. Wanting to give George as much pleasure as possible, he slowed his pace, lapping up and down slowly and dragging his tongue along the smooth length of his cock.

"Ah... Sirous... I..."

"Mm?"

He hummed lightly around the drake's cock, though blissful tension crackled between them. His shaft throbbed wantonly in Sirous' maw and George tried to keep his head from spinning, though he felt like he was going to lose control already.

Would that be embarrassing to spill his seed into Sirous' mouth so soon? It could have been, but it didn't feel at all like that would be the case with the red drake. He called on those vulnerable parts of him he didn't like to expose, yet it felt like everything could and would be okay with Sirous.

Even if it was a little awkward sometimes. He grunted in the back of his throat, pulling at Sirous' right horn, but he didn't want the dragon to stop. He just wanted to... change things up a little, his tail trying to lift even then.

Sirous did as he asked, a string of saliva connecting his lips to the dragon's cock as he pulled back, warm breath tickling the head of George's dick. But George wanted something more, licking his lips and giving Sirous a plaintive look.

"I..." He blushed heavily, the scales heating on his cheeks even more than before. "It's... I want you..."

"You have me."

"Want you...inside me."

Sirous grinned and rubbed the dragon's hip soothingly.

"That is something I very much can do for you... Roll on to your side for me, I'll take care of you, George."

George shivered, loving the sound of his name on Sirous' lips, though the drake was already moving swiftly, though he paused when it became clear he didn't have something required to get started. Pursing his lips, George lifted his tail and pointed towards his belongings set at the side of the room.

"There's…lube in the bag, inside pocket."

"You bring *lubricant* with you when travelling?" Sirous asked incredulously, though even he was unable to ignore how something in him pulled, warming to the notion of George thinking ahead for such a thing. "Well, I cannot say it won't be useful…"

He smiled and found the lube after only a little rummaging, using it to glide his hand over his cock. It gleamed with the hint of lube, where a little went a long way, and Sirous took care to drip a little of the thick fluid on to his fingers too, so he could take care of Sirous' tail hole before sliding deep, *deep* inside as he ached to.

The pucker of flesh resisted him briefly as he slid his fingers over it, gently nudging the dragon's tail up a little higher so everything he needed to reach was exposed. Gently, he allowed his fingers to lightly tease inside and slid them deep, testing how ready George was for him. He wasn't about to rush things, yet it already felt as if his cock was going to explode with lust, pleasure aching desperately through him.

But he would take his time, not worrying about his own needs as Sirous rocked his hips, grinding lightly back against him. There seemed to be an edge of uncertainty to him, although George kept his mouth shut, grunting and groaning through closed lips. Sirous' fingers pushed up deeper, working the lube within the dragon's tail hole, though he kept a close eye on his partner too.

"Let me know if anything is sore, if you need me to slow down, or if you want to stop," he said gently, wanting to remind George, especially then. "We don't have to do anything you don't want to do."

George cast him an annoyed yet needy look that almost had Sirous letting out a sharp bark of laughter that would not have fit the moment. His tail snaked around and clasped Sirous' tightly, draping heavily over Sirous' hip.

"No," he rasped, his voice deeper and much less refined. "I want you… Only you."

That could have meant so much more, but Sirous refused to listen to the frantic fluttering of his heartbeat in his chest. That was something he would address at a later date and time, his hand sliding free of George's rump as he lined up. The drake's wings shuffled against Sirous' chest, but there was more than enough room for him to spoon up behind George, his hard-on teasing over the scales of his rump to the tight yet lubed-up pucker of his anal ring.

Slowly, gently, he pressed the head of his cock to that ring, guiding himself in with the aid of his own hand. Yet it was all Sirous could do not to moan like a virgin as he shuddered against George, an inch more of his cock suddenly spearing into the dragon's backside than he'd intended. George gasped and squeezed around his length, though the dragon only ground back on that shaft, wanting to feel it more deeply, more intimately, despite the sudden stretch.

The ridges on Sirous' cock eased into his ass as George gasped and groaned, his tongue flickering against the side of his muzzle and lapping wetly back inside. With his eyes half-closed, he needed Sirous' hand on his leg, helping him lift it up and forward so Sirous could grind in more deeply, the squeeze of their tails around one another letting them know exactly where the other stood in the moment.

"Oh…" George moaned. "You feel…"

He wanted it all the more, more than he had ever thought he could. That hot length of dragon cock stretched him out slowly and yet he only wanted the full shaft buried inside him, perhaps even to be pinned under the red dragon and fucked until his head spun. Maybe that would come another time, though George didn't want his fantasies to get the better of him, fighting not to squeeze hard around the length powering up under his tail.

Yet Sirous seemed in tune with him as he rocked his hips and let George guide him on. The more George ground back against him, putting an arch into his lower back, the more Sirous pushed into him. He thrust a little harder, feeling his way deeper, yet the ridges grinding and teasing over George's anal ring had the dragon's cock leaking pre-cum, so close to exploding.

With the natural heat that resided within the body of a dragon, George's cock remained hard and throbbing as he was taken, though the drake didn't know whether it was to be counted as "making love" or a cruder, rougher "fuck." He didn't know what he wanted, for he longed for a bit of both – and could that be such when he was with Sirous?

It was impossible to tell so he leaned into the pleasure of the moment, forgetting all else. His poetry didn't matter, not all the other furs he'd associated with before: only Sirous. The dragon's hot breath rasped over his head and the back of his neck and he moaned, licking his lips, grinding with the drake and letting his body rock in time with Sirous' thrusts.

"Mmm… You are wonderful," Sirous hissed against the back of his head, pressing the tip of his nose between George's horns. "So…mmmph…tight… You feel amazing… You *are* amazing."

George blushed, but the heat in his face went unnoticed as Sirous let the motion of his hips pick up, keeping his cock a little deeper inside George so he didn't pull out very far with every stroke. The ridges pressed up deeply into his sensitive passage and George's hips bucked without the active consent of his mind, like the white-scaled dragon's body was no longer under his control.

But he had Sirous there to take care of him as he groaned and let pleasure roll through him, his cock dripping pre-cum on to the bed. Yet it would not be wasted as Sirous boldly reached around, his arm pressing into the drake's thigh to help keep it raised while closing his hand around his cock.

With George's moans, increasingly loud, filling the room, Sirous thrust with longer, more powerful strokes, focusing on the connection between them. He groaned and let passion lead him on, stroking up and down the length of George's shaft while he adored and memorised every inch of that smooth length. But he would have many times over to learn the curves of it, the feel of the head under his fingers and in his mouth, as the dragons grew closer, all in good time.

They would always remember that first time together, however, as Sirous ground in deeply, thrusting in short, driving strokes that made George moan so very sweetly, gasping and grabbing at breath. Yet his body convulsed and he rocked against Sirous, need coursing through him with the passion of a drake in the midst of flight. He couldn't hold back and neither did any part of him want to as his body quivered with delight, thrusting away from Sirous even as he wanted to push back against him, spending his seed on to the bed. Thick spurts of dragon cum poured from the head of his cock, cum marking his tip, though George was not present in his mind enough right then to care about how he looked.

All he could do was greedily take that shared pleasure, grunting and gasping, nostrils flared while Sirous growled and nipped at his neck. He couldn't help himself, not as that hand caressed him, sending him to pulse after pulse of a high he had not even come close to experiencing in, well…months if not years. But it was all he needed as Sirous nuzzled in close to him and pressed his chin over his shoulder, letting his chest press as flush to his back as he could.

Sirous revelled in the beauty of the drake languishing in orgasm, conscious of everything from the feel of his scales brushing up against his body to the rasp of heady breath in George's throat. It was the kind of thing he wanted to feel over and over again, all so he could savour the moment and get to come back to the white dragon's arms whenever he missed the feel of their bodies coming together.

Still, he wanted his high too and George had the presence of mind to grind his rump back against him, his tail pushed up all the way so Sirous could get as deep as their bodies allowed. Maybe there would be other positions they could try, to get even deeper, but that would have to come in the future.

He thrust harder, a near savage growl tearing itself from his lips. George moaned, begging for it, and he ached to give the drake every drop he yearned for. With a thrust of his hips and a rising throb of pleasure that could not and would not be denied, he let loose, ropes of slick cum shooting deep into George's tail hole. Ecstasy washed over him and Sirous moaned, shuddering in relief even as George pressed back against him, securing him in place with his presence alone.

Only time would tell just what was to come from that night together, their first meeting and, of course, their first time sleeping with one another. Sirous panted heavily, chest heaving against George, but he had to hold fast in the moment, releasing George's cock at last and wrapping his arm around as much of the drake as he could – which was rather a lot, with George's slight frame. Yet his cock still shot every drop of seed he could give deeply up inside the dragon's ass, a little rendering the join of their bodies slick, though little dripped out. He grunted, a whisper from George reaching his years, but the words were not quite decipherable.

That was no matter. Not as they shared in the moment, letting it all roll through them, to experience every drop, every second, like it mattered more than the one preceding it.

Slowly, as they came down from their high, sleep tugging at them, the drakes relaxed against one another. The dawn would find them in one another's arms under the covers, Sirous having tenderly scooted the white drake into bed, to make sure he wouldn't catch a chill in the night.

Dragons and their mead could go one of two ways. But, mostly, they ended up together.

With white scales and red scales laying over one another, enraptured by the promise of all that was to come, Sirous and George slumbered deeply, tails entwined. The poet and the adventurer found one another at exactly the point in time they were meant to, as was the way of fate.

a deep breath, puffing out his cheeks with air, and turned slowly.

Mist surrounded him. Damn it. He had no sense of his bearings, peering at the only scrubby bush that was in his range of vision, but it didn't give him any more information. He didn't know whether or not he'd passed it before, or if he had got turned around at any point.

Meic had just been trying to get up to Paxton's Tower, after visiting Castell Dryslwyn, but the mist that he'd been admiring sweeping down the valley had come in as if something was chasing it. It didn't move, at least to his eye, like normal mist, rolling and heaving at the front, as if a charging herd of white horses was leading the way.

Of course, he'd shrugged it off, thinking it was all a trick of his eyes, but he didn't know what to believe anymore. A deep cold sank into his bones and he shook his head, tugging the collar of his coat up further around his neck, though it didn't have the effect he wanted it to.

"Unff. I got to get out of here."

He had to get back to the car, one way or the other, but, frankly, Meic had no idea how that was even going to be possible. The mist surrounded him, swirling and drifting, moving as if with the fluidity of water.

He grunted, shaking his head. At least he could still breathe. That, at the very least, was something…

Meic's ear twitched, trying to shake off a drop of water. He paused, squinting at a patch of mist right there before him. It didn't look right, not as it darkened.

"What the…"

He took a step back, sniffing the air, a new scent reaching him. Yet even the scents of the world around him were muted with the damp, cloying effect of the mist, which dulled his ability to hear too.

There was something there, however, perhaps a someone – even if Meic would not have believed it even if he saw it with his own eyes. A low groan echoed through the mist and he pinned his ears as flat as they could go to his skull, cursing under his breath as he stumbled backwards.

The mist swirled and flowed, taking on some kind of shape before him. A shape that became increasingly solid, forming a long, elegant muzzle and a flowing, rippling mane and tail. The creature rising from the mist was entirely nude and yet the solidity of their transforming hooves bore into the lightly soft ground, indenting it. It was that more than anything else that told Meic they were real, even as his heart pounded and blood roared in his ears.

"What the hell is happening… No… No…"

But…yes? His jaw hung open and he froze, feeling that odd pressure of his hackles rising a little at the back of his neck. Meic licked his lips, fear getting the better of him, but he couldn't flee and didn't even dare look away as a beautiful, dappled-grey horse solidified in the air before him as if he had been there all along. His haunches had more dapples on them than the midsection of his body, his chest broad and male with darker nipples showing through a thin coat of equine hair. The arch of his neck rose gracefully to meet a defined, dished cheek and the stallion's dark eyes had an inviting, liquid quality to them.

He was, of course, evidently a stallion from the fold of a grey sheath at his crotch, though even Meic pulled his eyes away from that part of the strange horse before he got caught. He knew he had balls: that was more than enough for him when it came to staring at a stranger, most certainly.

Not far away, Meic was sure he could hear the burble of the river, the water lapping against the riverbank, but he didn't think he was going to find it anytime soon.

"What…" He breathed, taking a step back, the fox's heart hammering in his chest with enough force for him to feel it echoing through his bones. "*What* are you?"

Perhaps it was not the most eloquent question to ask of such an apparition, but the horse's eyes were already on him, a mischievous gleam in them that could not be mistaken for moonlight. Well, it could have been – if not for the mist swirling around them.

"Oh! Shwmae!" The equine anthro nickered with a low, sweeping bow that had his darker forelock flopping forward over his eyes. "Sut wyt ti?"

"Uh…"

Meic tried to steady himself, taking another step back on to softer ground and holding his arms out for balance. Despite the pounding of his heart and blood roaring in his ears, adrenaline pumping through the network of his body, he was out of place there, distorted from his own perception of reality.

And yet…the horse was there, with a smile on his face, approaching with a hand somewhat outstretched, though it was not quite as if he was reaching for Meic. Absurdly, the fox wondered for a moment if the strange being was trying to help him – but, no, that could not be so. That would be crazier than even his eyes playing tricks on him that made him question his own sanity.

How was he meant to reconcile with the fact that the other anthro had appeared from thin air? That wasn't right. That wasn't right at all. And they were speaking Welsh? In all fairness, the latter was probably the least surprising thing of all.

His tongue stuck to the roof of his mouth as he took a breath and tried to calm himself – but who was

Meic really fooling there? The mist swirled and parted a little, offering a hazy glimpse of dark trees with their boughs cutting through the silence, the mist pressing in on the fox's ears with its usual muting effect.

Still, the horse's ears twitched, waiting on a response as Meic cleared his throat with a gulp and a hacking, gurgling sound from his throat.

"Dydw i ddim yn siarad Cymraeg," the fox tried with an apologetic shrug. "Uh… Ah, damn it."

"Oh!"

The horse laughed, a sharp sound that was cut off too quickly with the soft mist swirling around them. A bluish light filtered through, allowing greater definition to be pulled into the horse's features. Meic shivered, a ripple curling down his spine. Was it wrong of him to notice how handsome the horse was? The broadness of his chest seemed to go on forever, with sculpted shoulders too that drew his eye.

"Ah, sorry," the horse said, speaking English. "I did not think! There are few who come out this way at this time of day."

"Oh… Hm…"

Meic swallowed and rubbed the back of his neck, his heartbeat slowing somewhat, ears pricked. It didn't look like he was losing his mind, but maybe the mist had just swirled in such a way that he had *thought* the stallion had formed from the moisture in the air. That would be a far more feasible explanation for what was happening out there.

The fact that the dappled stallion was naked, however, was something he didn't think was normal, even if he didn't exactly hike all that much as it was. He was fairly sure something like a "naked ramblers" walk would be well-advertised due to laws around public nudity, but even Meic could not be sure about that.

"I don't really know what to say to that," Meic confessed, the fox deciding to go for honesty as the ground squidged under his shoes. "What… Why are you out here? Are you *naked*?"

"Oh!"

The stallion nickered and laughed again, running his fingers back through his mane. However, the strands seemed to ripple and flow as he caressed them, not holding the same form that typical hair may have done. The hairs on the back of Meic's neck prickled, hackles striving to raise, even though, with anthros, the shift of them was nowhere near as obvious as with ferals.

"I didn't even think of it, no one usually comes out this way past Castell Dryslwyn," he said, though he didn't seem all that bothered by the fox. "Are you quite okay?"

He didn't answer the fox's questions, but the horse smiled, seeing how his words led him on smoothly. It was the way of him, even though there was really no harm in the equine, not like with others of his kind.

Meic shifted his weight and pressed his lips together.

"Yes, yes… I'm fine, I'm okay," he said, though the fox took a breath, not really all that certain about it. "I'm just lost. The mist came in so quickly…and, look, all this is really weird. Who are you? What are you?"

"Oh, just the questions I was waiting for!"

The stallion laughed, joy in his heart, light on his hooves as he turned with a spinning motion, his mane and tail flowing like mist given a partially solid form behind him. The fox's eyes narrowed and his tail stiffened, but that didn't stop the stallion from completing his little presentation. It was all about show, after all.

"I am Llewelyn," he said with a smile. "You might know of the legends of these parts…but many call us water horses."

Meic gulped.

"Uh… Nice to meet you?" That seemed like the right thing to say, but Meic could not be sure. "I'm… I'm Meic. Like it sounds. Wait…"

His muzzle wrinkled as he adjusted his stance, instinct helping him ease into a mildly defensive position with a little bend in his knees, his left leg further forward than his right. The fox's ears twitched, though Meic had enough sense about him not to pin them in threat, for that was a common thread of body language between equines and vulpines.

"A water horse," he said slowly, sounding the words out as if he was coming to his own conclusion about matters. "Like…a kelpie?"

"I am not so common as a kelpie," Llewelyn huffed, tail swishing. "Ceffyl dŵr have far more to offer than those wretches."

"So, you don't tempt anthros to ride you and then plunge them into the depths of lakes when you toss them from your backs?"

Llewelyn paused.

"Well, not anymore…" He said with a roll of his eyes. "There are still some ceffyl dŵr, of course, that follow the old ways, but I am not one of them."

This is crazy… I'm losing my mind.

Meic shook his head.

"How am I supposed to believe that?" He growled, ears tipping back a little further. "I don't know that you're not here to hurt me and I've already said too much. I just want to go home, damn it!"

The outburst lunged from him as he clenched a paw into a fist. The horse blinked at him and approached more softly, lips moving as if he was chewing something.

"Please, I intended no offence and I didn't mean to scare you," Llewelyn said more gently. "There's just so few to talk to – you can already see I don't look like every other horse you've seen. Others… They usually run from me. I would assume it's only the mist here that has kept you from running."

Meic let out a short bark of humourless laughter, tension not leaving his body.

"Well… Yes, I was trying to get back to where I parked my car, but I doubt I'd even be able to get home without GPS right now."

Llewelyn's ears pricked and he smiled.

"That's something I can help with," he offered. "Look, I'll prove to you I'm here, that I'm solid, just for your sanity, of course. And I'll take you back to where you've parked your car, so you can get home too. No tricks."

Meic studied the horse, shoulders dropping a little.

"Even if I wasn't half-convinced that you're just a weirdo out here trying to trick people," Meic said, "I'm not sure how you're going to prove to me that you're real."

Llewelyn grinned.

"Touch me."

"What?" The fox yelped, startled so much so that the cry burst from his lips before he could restrain himself. "You can't be serious!"

"What – no!" The horse laughed, half bending over and neighing as his nostrils flared, too caught up in his own amusement to see the hot rush of embarrassment clawing at Meic's muzzle and cheeks. "No, not *that*! My arm, my chest: something like that.

You can touch other parts of me if you want too though, fox."

Meic clamped his jaw shut and shook his head, ears splayed shyly.

"Uh… Yeah, I got the wrong end of the stick there."

It was surreal, his stomach churning with embarrassment that didn't really belong there, staring at the equine so hard that his eyes watered a little. How could he say something like that? But he had been staring at the stallion and eyeing up his biceps in a way that was not proper in the slightest.

"I don't mind," Llewelyn said, as if he read Meic's mind. "You can look as much as you want."

"I wasn't looking!"

Meic growled and shook his head, tucking his tail down while trying to make it less obvious. The mist around him didn't seem so chilly anymore, not even as he shifted his weight from one foot to the other, skin prickling.

"Okay, so can you take me back to the car park then?" He said instead, changing the topic. "I want to go home, whatever the hell is going on here."

Llewelyn's nostrils flared and puckered almost sadly, nodding with a gentle tilt of his chin. If Meic wasn't imagining things, he'd have sworn the stallion appeared at least somewhat disappointed, but that surely could not be so.

"Of course," the stallion said smoothly, as if nothing had happened at all. "It is not all that far away"

Meic grimaced.

"That figures… It's so easy to get turned around in the mist."

"Undoubtedly."

The stallion brightened up again and turned slowly in a circle, the mist clinging to him like a flowing, sensual second skin. Meic could not help but watch, fascinated, as his mane and tail rippled and pulled, caught by an unseen wind. But maybe the horse really was of another world, another place and time. Perhaps Meic was not the kind of fox who was rooted in reality, but could allow himself to be tempted by another world.

He didn't know, but it was still hypnotising to watch the stallion, admiring his body, even down to the rise of his glutes. His tail lifted, as if he was trying to show off, but Meic managed to avert his eyes just in time. He didn't want to be caught staring at *that part* of the horse, after all!

Or did he? The fox rumbled a growl and shook it off. No, no… He'd have the horse, Llewelyn, take him back to the car park and, whatever the hell was happening there, he'd be out and home soon enough. Maybe he wouldn't go out hiking when the weather was closing in again, though he had thought that would be more of a problem higher in the mountains.

"Look how the world moves around us," Llewelyn breathed, as if he was experiencing the moment in another way, without Meic even being there. "We're a part of it and not. Anthros are so separate from their roots, the flow of water around them. Even those with wings – how often do they seem to soar?"

Meic swallowed hard. Damn, why was the stallion's voice so tantalising? He wanted to splay his hands out on Llewelyn's chest, pressing deep, sinking into the embodiment of the stallion in any way he could.

Maybe I just haven't got laid in a while.

"Come on then," Llewelyn said, extending his hand to the fox again, but he curled his fingers in an encouraging gesture, wanting the fox to follow him. "Let's get going, if you're not here for the show."

Meic blinked, but followed the horse with a sigh of relief that really had no place in his chest, the wet sound of the ground under his shoes catching his attention.

"Thanks… But what show are you talking about?"

The horse looked back at Meic over his shoulder and the fox kept his eyes up, trying not to follow the hypnotic swish of the stallion's tail.

"The night sky, the river bubbling away," he said casually. "Don't you ever just sit and watch the world go by?"

Meic opened his mouth to say something – and then the stallion was right in front of him, hands raised but no contact being made. Against himself, the fox squeaked, faced with the horse's lusciously broad chest, though Meic didn't step back. He didn't want to admit it, but a part of him was captivated, already in the ceffyl dŵr's thrall, though he was fortunate in that nothing bad would come to him as a result of that. There were many who had come across Llewelyn's kind who faced far worse fates from the darker tricksters.

Llewelyn, however, was a different kind. He smiled as the fox put his paws in his hands, seeming surprised that the horse really did have a solid form, the warmth of the vulpine intoxicating in the best of ways.

Oh, it was so good to have a warm body against him again and Llewelyn took a step back, holding Meic's paws. The fox moved right along with him as if they were dancing – and maybe they were. Everything came with that sense of lightness and grace to Llewelyn, but it was rare that a mere mortal would join him in his cavorting.

"I'm glad I found you out here, Meic," he said softly, his voice little more than a whisper through the reeds. "Having the company… It is a revelation. One day, perhaps, I could see myself integrating with the anthro world more, moving away from the river and Dryslwyn, so I can at least have a little more company."

"Oh…" Meic considered that for a moment, moving with the stallion as he allowed himself to be drawn in, very lightly, against the horse's chest. "Well… I guess that's why you're all creepy and stuff, appearing from the mist."

"I could ask for a favour though," Llewelyn suggested, a hopeful twinkle in his eye. "In payment for taking you to the car park. I'm going to get you out anyway, but…it would be nice."

Meic blushed and made as if to pull away, but it was as if he had already thrown caution to the wind. His hackles had softened and he sucked in a shuddering breath, his tail swinging back and forth more freely. Any trace of unwanted tension had left his body and he let the horse close his arms around him, his hands sweeping down the fox's back.

"I think it might be something I want even if you're not phrasing it as a favour."

The words tumbled past the fox's lips before he had a chance to control himself or call them back. Meic wasn't even sure he wanted to, for the less sensible part of his mind was warm and tingly, wanting to press up to the stallion who was not really like any kind of equine he'd been with before. Not in that way, not when he'd been staring avidly at the stallion for so long already, his need lurking and pushing in the back of his mind while he tried not to give in. Maybe it was the lure of a water horse of the Welsh mountains, or perhaps it was just something innate in Meic himself. Unless they continued, neither ceffyl dŵr nor fox would have any way at all of knowing.

So, when the stallion tipped Meic's chin up, their bodies pressed against one another, the fox went along with it. Llewelyn's nose tipped down sensually and he kissed Meic softly, though the chaste kiss was not to last. It deepened swiftly as liquid need pooled in the fox's loins, desire arcing up passionately as his sheath plumped out.

It should have been embarrassing for the fox, to be enticed so swiftly by a creature of the mist, but could anyone really have blamed him? Not when he was faced with that seductively muscled chest and the shoulders he yearned to kiss, letting his lips brush over each spot while memorising every inch of the stallion's body. Llewelyn was different, very much so, yet the fox tried to frame it in his mind as him "falling prey" to the water horse's "trap," even if he was very much in charge of his own senses.

It was his decision, even if there was a part of Meic that sincerely thought he was losing his mind. It was not at all like him to give in to desire, even when there was a hard length of horse cock pushing from Llewelyn's sheath, teasing up against his abdomen. His heart lurched and he moaned into the stallion's mouth, kissing him more and more deeply, their tongues sweeping lusciously up against one another as the fox gave leave to anything that may have held him back.

It was better to sink into the moment, to let the magic of the mist and the relief of being saved flow through him. And the equine was so very solid against him as he groaned into his mouth, feeling those soft lips move against his own in the best of ways. The stallion drew him backwards with him, until Llewelyn's knees folded and he sat on a large rock, though it was a good height for him with his hooves still flat on the ground. Meic ended up sitting in his lap, blushing heavily, as the stallion pushed his jacket back from his shoulders, baring the red fur of his arms.

Meic allowed himself to be undressed, head spinning in an almost pleasant fashion. It should have been too much for him, all too quickly, yet the fire of lust inside him could not be softened so swiftly. He tried to keep contact with the stallion even as his T-shirt was drawn up and over his head, though the fox did not even shiver in the cooler air.

It was too hot, his skin prickling in the best of ways, grunting in the back of his throat as he dipped his nose and kissed the stallion's chest, lips moving over his short coat as muscles shifted under his touch. He felt the horse's chest rising against him in a sharp intake of breath and the fox smirked subtly to himself. Despite everything, he was coming to terms with how different the horse and he were – and Meic still managed to draw such a reaction from him.

Maybe we are more alike than I thought.

Or enough so that they could meet one another halfway, Llewelyn helping the fox to stand so he could tug at his jeans, pulling them down slowly. Meic moaned his consent, giving a little rocking push of his hips to help ease them down, though getting his shoes off (luckily he had not bothered wearing socks) was the most difficult point. The warmth of Llewelyn's lips on Meic's swept away any embarrassment that could have arisen from the awkwardness of that moment, clutching at the stallion as if he needed to keep kissing him for the sake of life itself.

Llewelyn's heart sang as he ran his hand down the fox's body, gently stroking his abs muscles, although they were a little more hidden by the red and white fur of his body than his own muscles were. He'd not been so close with another, who was not of his kind, for so long – and it somehow felt like he had been meant to meet the fox out there. He hadn't wanted to hide away in the slightest from him, despite usually lurking in the water when there were visitors out there, not partaking in trickery like his kind.

Llewelyn just wanted the fox, need rising as his thickening member throbbed between them. It was a good few inches longer than Meic's, but that was not the point, not even as the fox's paws found his shaft too, squeezing the length, running over it. Llewelyn liked to think the fox was trying to capture every inch and edge of his body as he was trying to do with Meic, but the moment pulled them along, like water rushing downstream, eager to reach the ocean.

"You…" He breathed, marvelling at the moment, his hand around the back of the fox's head, stroking his fur and the patch behind his ears. "You are amazing… How could I be so lucky?"

Meic moaned, though he didn't quite know how to reply to that, as if the stallion was stealing words from his lips. He kind of wanted to say that aloud, but he wasn't sure how the horse would react – so he let himself lean into the moment instead. His paws caressed that throbbing length of horse cock as his fingers slid over the medial ring. There was no way, surely, he could take that inside him, not like that – or was Llewelyn so magical that he could surpass even that barrier?

He rather liked the thought of that, but the equine slowly but firmly slid down before him to his knees. It somehow seemed wrong to him for the horse to be the one down on his knees, but Meic still enjoyed the view, his fingers trying to tangle with the horse's mane. The taste of the stallion lingered on his lips and he let out a soft, puff of breath, the horse's lips meeting the head of his own tapered cock.

"Ah… Oh, wow…"

He moaned openly as the horse's lips parted to succulently take his cock into his mouth. The equine's broad, fleshy tongue, caressed the underside as need lurched within the fox's body, wanting more even then. Yet he had to pace himself, for he didn't want to cum too quickly, no. He wanted to drag it out, to savour the moment, to let every little thing play out exactly as it was supposed to.

Even if he was out there in the open, whimpering and moaning, a ceffyl dŵr sucking down his cock all the way to the base as he bobbed his head on it.

Meic couldn't quite grasp Llewelyn's mane, however, as the horse lapped around the head of his cock, swirling his tongue around the tip of the fox's shaft and teasing every sensitive spot he could find there. But the fox couldn't quite grip on to the stallion's ethereal mane, his attention dragged away from it even as it flittered and danced between his fingers.

It was easier to focus on how good those lips felt on his cock, sliding up and down with that tongue adding more saliva. The stallion slurped lewdly on his red shaft, lips breaking from the head for a single, heaving breath of a moment, a string of saliva connecting Llewelyn's lips to Meic's shaft.

And then it broke, though the spell was still in place, still holding them close. The horse looked up at the fox, trying to maintain eye contact with the bluish glow of the mist behind him: the veil between the worlds. It was not natural, yet Meic had somehow walked right into it, even as twilight fell, and he lapped sensually at the fox's cock, wanting him to quiver under his touch.

It was as if it had electrified the fox and Meic exhaled hotly, tongue flicking out from between his lips and sweeping against the side of his muzzle. He rocked his hips without thinking about what he was doing, heat crawling through him. Need pooled within him and he had to push through it, to remember he didn't want to let loose right away, no. He had to be bolder, had to hold back for at least a little longer, for he didn't want to cum quickly.

It was about letting the moment be all that it was and not expecting anything more of it. Meic moaned as the stallion dived right back on to his cock, pursing his lips tightly around the fox's member and having no qualms at all about sliding all the way down. Meic whimpered as his knot pulsed at the base, not yet fully formed but slowly trying to plump up. How could the equine hit all the right notes for him even when they had not been together before?

He didn't have to worry about that, however, not as he moaned and rolled his hips forward, thrusting a little into the stallion's mouth. Llewelyn's tongue chased his length, twisting partly around his cock, even though a horse's tongue was not the kind that could wrap around a shaft, like that of a reptile's. But everything about the ceffyl dŵr grounded him there, as if every muscular twitch and tingle in his body had been pulled into stark definition, breath clawing at his chest as he heaved for it.

"Ah… Llewelyn…"

Meic tried to catch the stallion's attention, though it took a few moments for him to look up, his eyes hazy with desire. His own hard-on had not been given anywhere near as much attention as Meic's had been, although the fox wanted to change that.

"Hm?"

Llewelyn blinked as he was drawn up, slowly, finding himself standing and then sitting back on the rock. He grunted for breath, chest juddering with every lungful of air, though it should not have been so difficult for him. And then there was a fox climbing into his lap again, knees sliding to either side of his hips despite the sure discomfort they had to face, kneeling on the stone.

Yet he couldn't bring himself to ease Meic off him as their eyes met and the fox whimpered throatily, hips raising as the stallion grasped his cock in one hand. He pointed his shaft up, letting the head rub gently in the crease of the fox's butt, seeking his tail hole. When he felt the pucker on the tip of his length, he pulled Meic down slowly, the fox's tight hole straining around him, gripping his shaft fervently as Meic took more and more of his cock inside his ass.

The fox's tongue lolled out and he huffed, heaving for breath.

"Ah… Yes…"

It was euphoric, his own cock somehow remaining hard through it all, pre-cum beading at the head. It did not break from the tip, however, remaining perfectly in place as the equine's shaft pushed up deeply inside him, though it was Meic who was completely and utterly in control of his own motions. The fox moaned openly and licked his lips, only to have them captured by the ceffyl dŵr, his heart pounding.

Bliss swam through him, the fox trying to rock his hips even as Llewelyn stopped him from grinding down too far too quickly. Yet there was little either fox or stallion had to worry about in the heat of the moment as Meic's tail hole stretched past the medial ring, taking the thicker span of the horse's shaft deep. Meic quivered, kissing the stallion back with due passion, though it was a wet, messy sort of kiss, saliva coating their lips and a gleam of drool at the corner of the fox's.

Llewelyn's heart jumped and thudded almost painfully in his chest, pulling the fox close even as the swell of his cock made a light bulge through Meic's lower abdomen. His tail flicked, but he was more focused on making sure the fox did not slip from him, for that would have been a bump he very much did not want to see Meic get.

Yet the stallion's heart leapt and he kissed the fox desperately, hungry for something in the closeness of their bodies that he did not honestly feel he'd been able to have before. It had been too isolated out there, not meshing with his fellow water horses, yet Llewelyn could not consider all that as the moment wrapped around them. The mist swirled, opening up their surroundings just a little more, his cock throbbing insistently, demanding its needs were met, inside the fox's tail hole.

Such a tight hole like that had no business in clenching and pulling around him as divinely as it was, his shaft aching and pulsating with need. Llewelyn let out a needy grunt into Meic's mouth, but he wanted to hold back just a little longer, despite the thrumming of his own need. The head of his cock puffed up, flaring lightly inside the fox's tight passage, yet he tensed his abs and glutes, contracting every muscle he could as he squeezed Meic tightly to him.

Meic, however, moaned and broke the kiss, twisting and rocking his hips fervently. He pushed down roughly on the stallion's cock, taking as much of his length into his ass as he felt it was possible to do. The stretch was incredible, blistering through him with a throbbing swell of heat that shot straight to his cock. There was no denying that push of passion, how it ached within him. With his cock throbbing between them, bowed lightly up against the horse's stomach, he howled brokenly as pleasure shot through him.

His lust poured from him in devious spurts of seed, splattering over their bodies, though any mess would be swiftly washed off afterwards: hardly something either of them had to worry about. Llewelyn bowed his head over the fox's shoulder with a needy huff, Meic's head swimming with desire. Yet the fox had everything his body needed right there in the moment and the stallion thrust up, spearing an inch more of his member into the vulpine.

It was all he needed as his balls ached and churned, erupting with an outpouring of his lust. There was no stopping the flow of his seed as it splattered up into the fox, very little trickling and drooling back out from the join of their bodies. The seal of his cock within the fox's tight rump was simply too devout, as if their coming together was another kind of bond they would carry with them forevermore.

He huffed and leaned over the fox, pressing his head down, eyes half-closed. There was nothing more for it than for Llewelyn to lean into the moment, his shoulders rounding lightly as he held on to Meic as if for life itself. Every throb of his cock sent more and more cum shooting up into the fox's ass, yet it was so much more than the crude exultation of the moment – but that would only come to be seen between them as their relationship brought them closer and closer.

Meic, blinking through the aftershocks of bliss, the stallion's cock still hard inside him, pulled back. His nose brushed the horse's cock and Llewelyn nickered a response, sitting back enough so he could look to Meic with one eye.

"I think…" He breathed heavily, chest rising and falling sharply for needy, near savage, grabs of air. "I think…I should go home. We should go home."

Llewelyn's cheeks warmed, though his dark grey coat hid his blush.

"There's nothing I'd like more."

Meic grinned foolishly and, again, the two kissed, though it was softer and more drawn out that time. Their tongues brushed together more tenderly as Llewelyn's cock softened slowly inside him, a drool of cum marking the base where it leaked from Meic's strained pucker. Yet the moment was for them and them alone, no matter for the mist closing in once more; Meic no longer had any fear of that. How could he when he felt as sweetly settled in his chest as he did, like something he'd been waiting for had eased into place?

With Llewelyn leading the way in front of his car, the ceffyl dŵr shapeshifting into a quadrupedal equine form to better leap and gallop along the road, Meic was guided safely home. He was not a victim of the mischievous water horses of Wales, though Llewelyn's brethren shook their heads at his antics, seeing him finally leaving them as he had said he was going to do so many times over.

Yet Llewelyn had found someone who gave him the motivation and energy to get out, to find a new way. He might not have it all figured out, but, frankly, the ceffyl dŵr did not need to.

With Meic, he no longer needed to cavort, to flit through the mist and the river, easing between worlds. For him, the world had opened up. And, for Meic, something had slotted into place inside him he'd never quite thought he would find.

In exactly the right moment, two souls destined for each other had come together in the most magical of ways.

A Wolf's Hunger

Cynwyd, in Denbighshire, was a typically sleepy village in the Welsh mountains, but it was where Alec's family were from, even though the golden-furred hare had moved to the Midlands in England some time ago. Still, it was thankfully not all that far for him to travel, even if he swore the last part of the drive, when he headed deeper into the mountains down roads that twisted and wound, seemed to cling to the valley sides in fear of the tumbling drops they may otherwise have faced. The trip to see close family was all the better when he had someone with him to share the drive.

The slim, tall hare thrust his paws deep into his pockets as he headed out of town and towards the bridge that spanned the River Dee. Darkness had fallen after having dinner out in the pub with his parents and his senses were pleasantly fuzzy around the edges, his gait a little uneven where it should normally have been smooth and fluid. His long legs had branded him as a runner from a young age, but, truthfully, Alec was more interested in playing video games than engaging in many sports. Hiking, however – now that was more interesting. Yet he'd had someone else to spark his interest in that too and that, at least, would forever be a positive notion.

However, the village had a strange air to it after dusk, the trill of birdsong dying down as they settled down to roost for the night. A barn owl screeched nearby and his tall ears stood up straight, the hare's nose twitching as his whiskers quivered. Yet there was nothing for them to sense on the air – nothing a body like his would pick up on, anyway.

He walked a little more swiftly, ducking his head against a chilling wind, stirring up fallen leaves from the side of the bridge, though the bridge itself was clear. Oddly so, even, the hare pausing for a breath before continuing as dark clouds swirled, allowing glimpses of moonlight and starlight to spill over the land.

It wasn't much further, he told himself, though something inside the hare urged him to turn back – to return to the lights and safety and warmth of the pub and village. It would be easier to go back to his parents and find security there, while something inside him told Alec he was walking straight into danger.

He took a breath, steadying himself, yet it didn't really do all that much. His tail twitched, itching to flip up in a warning signal, but he could tuck his tail within his clothes far more easily than other anthros, like dogs, could. Still, it wiggled and pushed against the inside of his smarter, darker jeans, the heavy fabric feeling tight and restrictive where he knew he could not have stretched out into his full stride if he needed to.

The wind picked up and Alec reached the centre of the bridge, clouds scudding away from the moon to cast a silvery glow over the river. Beneath the bridge, the River Dee rushed by, full of rainwater and hastening its path towards the ocean. It would not be halted by any kind of "suspicious feeling" a hare had and most certainly not the anxious tightening in Alec's chest that made him want to take a deep, full breath – yet restricted such at the same time. He freed his paws without thinking about what he was doing, needing them out on pure instinct, just in case.

A screech, faint, reached his pricked, tall ears and the hare paused, glancing around. The bed of the river was rocky and muddied more singular sounds that reached his ears, which only added to his sense of unease. He hesitated, a triangular passing-place allowing him to slip to the side. Once, they were intended to allow those on foot to move out of the way of carriages, but the bridge was then used for pedestrians and light traffic in a modern day and age.

There may have been no cars out that night, but he didn't feel like he could go any further.

His skin prickled and the hare set his shoulders back, eyes wide and unblinking. Alec stared into the darkness, lips slightly parted, yet swallowing the saliva pooling in his mouth would not satisfy his dry throat in the slightest.

"Maelgwn, I *know* you're there."

"Aw, you're no fun."

A shadow moved, as if the wall of the bridge itself was unfurling, and Alec stepped back with a sigh and a puff of exhaled breath he had not realised his body needed so badly to release. A pair of red eyes that seemed to blaze with a hellish fire rose to at least depict where his head was, though the definition of his wolf-ish, masculine muzzle was still hidden by the cloak of night. Of course, the wolf anthro deigned to face the moonlight, allowing his features to remain cast into shadow.

The wolf stood tall, at least six inches taller than the hare – but that wasn't taking Alec's ears into account. Such things could be deceptive and yet the dark-furred wolf had so very perfectly blended into the bridge and surrounding landscape that Alec was sure he could have walked right past him if he had not called the wolf out on his usual shenanigans. But what else could he really expect from Y Gwyllgi?

Y Gwyllgi were not all that familiar to Alec when he'd first met the wolf in a bar back in England, drinking happily on an university night out. Maelgwn had been trying to find a new way in life – though the dark wolves and hounds still lived normal enough lives where they were to be found. Only, they seemed to face more difficulties than anthros without a mythical edge to them, something that made them "other" and separated them from the rest of the anthros in the world. Most Y Gwyllgi were canine, but they had been known to be foxes and, of course, wolves too.

Y Gwyllgi could be harmless or malignant, though that was true of any anthro in the world, regardless of their ability to slip into the shadows, blending with the environment as if they were slipping between two realities. They tended to startle and frighten others more, however, and had a bad habit of turning up at crossroads or empty roads at night. In rural areas, that was often in the depths of the countryside, perhaps with creaking, age-old trees framing the road with knowledge in their boughs, but they could just as easily be found uncomfortably in dark alleyways in towns and cities too. As the world had expanded and grown, the lives of Y Gwyllgi had integrated, even if they were different.

Maelgwn had that inclination to frighten and, unsurprisingly, Alec's boyfriend worked in the horror film industry, though thankfully in editing and special effects (he had multiple interests) rather than as an actor. As much as Alec might have loved jetting off on location with the dark-furred wolf, he would have missed his partner a lot more if he was into directing, acting or anything that would have required him to be on-site. Virtual meetings at odd hours, however, were occasionally the bane of their life.

"You seem to know where I am whatever I do," the dark wolf said with an approving nod, turning a little so the hare could see his lips parting and tongue lolling out in a casual grin. "You're getting better…"

"I know you said you were going to walk me back, *dog*," Alec teased, his tone lighter, "but you didn't have to sneak up on me like that. I take it you're feeling a little better then?"

Maelgwn nodded and flicked his tail, which protruded through the anthro-modified pair of jeans he was wearing, though they were dark like his fur. In keeping with Maelgwn's usual inclinations, the wolf wasn't wearing anything on his top half, his broad chest bare and pecs defined through even his thicker fur. That spoke volumes as to his level of fitness and muscle building, but Alec would have preferred to see the wolf in all his glory in better lighting.

"Not a dog," Maelgwn quipped back, lips twitching at the playful insult. "But, yes, I am feeling better. I don't know what it was about the drive that took it out of me!"

"To think of it," Alec laughed, stepping in close to Maelgwn and letting his body lay against the wolf's, leaning into his cool sense of solidity and safety. "A *wolf* then, Y Gwyllgi, still thrown off by a little car sickness!"

Maelgwn grunted and grabbed the hare, spinning him around so his back was to the stone wall of the bridge. Tucked into one of the triangular passing places, the hare gasped, though Alec's heart pounded in a far more familiar way as the wolf bore him back, the wall just about low enough to balance him. Alec had no fear, however, that the wolf would let him fall. He was yet to see the full scope of Maelgwn's powers, as the wolf developed his knowledge and moved through his innate abilities more easily with experience, but Alec was sure catching him from plummeting into the water was well within Maelgwn's range already.

Still, Alec wouldn't have wanted to take an untimely tumble as he held on to the wolf, even if Maelgwn held him close, refusing to allow even a breath of space between their bodies. Alec's body bowed back as Maelgwn pressed over him, the wolf's paws sliding down to his lower back.

"Mmm… But Y Gwyllgi must hunt, hare," he breathed, the cool of his breath tickling Alec's white whiskers. "I want you…"

Alec sucked in a breath, though it came out in a rush only a moment later. His heart thudded in his chest and he licked his lips, though Maelgwn was close to him, that muzzle and head blocking his view of the moon. He didn't need it to see, however, not as he breathed in the wolf's scent.

It rendered him dizzy, that overwhelming masculinity swelling through, a pulse of something dark and oaken with a hint of spice. Underneath it all was the wolfish musk that belonged to Maelgwn and Maelgwn alone, though the hare was most used to becoming lost in it in the privacy of their shared bedroom.

"Ah, Maelgwn," he grunted, forcing the words out through clenched teeth. "What are you doing?"

"Mm, what does it look like I'm doing?"

The wolf grinned, showing a flash of white teeth for only a breath of a moment, his pink tongue snaking out casually against the side of his muzzle. It flicked and dragged against his snout and the hare drew back slightly, the part of him that was still prey sensing the power of a predator so close to him. Yet it was something he'd learned to live with, for it was all worth it to be with a true predator, someone who held power and yet wielded it with care and grace, merely interested in living his life.

"You..." Alec's breath hitched in his throat, feeling like there was a lump there, or something tightening. "You... We can't, not out here."

The wolf's eyes sparkled darkly, inviting the hare into their hypnotising depths.

"Oh? Why is that?"

Maelgwn had always been a wolf of few words and Alec hissed through his teeth, trying to come to his senses. Yet what was it about the wolf that seemed to sweep them entirely from him, as if they had never existed in the first place? It was too easy to be pulled into the wolf's arms, pinned to his muscular, protective frame, yet his body already tingled in anticipation of what was to come.

He didn't really want to stop, after all, even as he looked back and forth while the wolf's muzzle trailed down to his neck, nipping and licking playfully while Alec suppressed a needy moan. He checked, weakly, to make sure there was no one approaching, that no one was heading back that way to the rental cottage they had for a long weekend there. There were rooms above the pubs in the village, but the two of them had wanted a little more privacy, so the cottage across the river had fit the bill perfectly instead.

It wasn't far…and yet Alec simply didn't have the desire to head back to it anymore, not as he grunted and the wolf's teeth passionately grazed his neck.

His breath caught, heartbeat fluttering, yet the innate wariness of a prey animal tangled with arousal. Alec sucked in a breath as the wolf's long, pink tongue bathed his neck, playing down the vulnerable expanse as Maelgwn grunted and lifted his tail. Delightful tension lined the wolf's body, yet it was all as if he was "hunting" Alec still, the hare nothing more than something to be devoured and longed for.

Yet Maelgwn had the hare exactly where he wanted him, even though Alec had not yet responded. His consent was in the gleam of his eyes, the rock of his hips against Maelgwn, though the wolf kept his ears pricked to catch any hint of the hare's discomfort. There was no harm in pushing boundaries gently, such as getting frisky in a riskier location, but he didn't want to truly impose on Alec in any way at all.

The hare, however, shuddered against him and the hard rise of his shaft begged attention, teasing against the front of his jeans while the wolf let his body press against Alec's. He teased gently, rolling his hips, though Maelgwn was still taller than the hare and Alec whimpered as his shaft was pleased lightly.

"Mmph… Mael…" He breathed, eyes glassy with lust. "More… Please…"

"Oh, I love hearing my name on your lips," the wolf growled, his paw at the hare's button and zipper, fiddling to get them released. "Say it again."

Alec quivered. The wolf knew *exactly* how to get to him and he loved it.

"Maelgwn."

"Mm, that's right."

Maelgwn wasted no time, the wolf's blood singing with desire as he freed the button and zip, pulling the latter down on Alec's jeans. His underwear was the next challenge, only exacerbated by the fact Alec preferred wearing boxer briefs. They were form-fitting and made the hare's ass look utterly fantastic, round and fuckable, but they did sometimes make sliding them down a little more challenging in "other" locations.

There, they had to be quiet, taking their leave and liberty of one another quickly. Hasty kisses were exchanged, the wolf's lips crushed warmly to Alec's as he crouched a little, his body longing to be close. The hare's slim frame fit into him perfectly and the wolf groaned, grasping his hip so he could grind into Alec. His cock slid a little high, the bulge in Maelgwn's pants impossible to ignore, but the wolf held back while he riled up Alec even more.

His paw worked quickly, relieving the pressure in his jeans and pants with a flick of his paw that unbuckled his jeans, catching and popping the button free. With Maelgwn's aching erection demanding attention, swelling from his sheath, he let his cock spring loose, thick and throbbing, a gleam of pre-cum smeared across the tapered head. Alec moaned.

"Please…"

"What are you asking for, hare?" Maelgwn teased. "This? Or maybe this?"

He kissed the hare roughly again, his tongue lustfully invading Alec's mouth. It swirled around and around, not allowing the hare to get an edge on him, but that was exactly the dynamic they liked. It was better with hot, rushed breaths hissing into one another and the wolf's paw sliding around the hare's cock, which bobbed free in the air with his balls still tucked back behind the hem of his underwear. As much as Maelgwn would have liked to squeeze and tease them too, that would have to wait for another time together – and there would be plenty of that to come, he was sure of it.

The hare rolled his hips beautifully against him as he stroked his cock, teasing him with a light grip and not quite giving Alec what he wanted. Alec pressed back against the cold stone, although even that seemed to warm a little to the heat of his body, his tail twitching and failing to relieve any of the delightful tension to be found there.

His heart surged and his ears folded back, head spinning pleasantly. How could Maelgwn hit all the right spots with him time after time again? Being with the wolf felt like he was slipping into the space between realities too, though he never quite knew where Maelgwn went when he eased into the shadows. Maybe it was just Alec's mortal eyes that couldn't catch the dark of the wolf, or perhaps Maelgwn had more secrets to reveal, but he'd be right there for each and every one.

The wolf's paw on his cock felt too good, pre-cum lightly dribbling from the tip in a wet gleam.

Maelgwn groaned into Alec's mouth and the hare moaned in turn, begging without words for what would make his blood hotter than ever. He could have been back in the cottage with Maelgwn on top of him, pinning him into the mattress while his cock drove deep into his tail hole – yet that was perhaps a little too much for being out on the bridge with the water rushing by below.

"Mmm…" He groaned, breaking the kiss, though the wolf's lips and teeth worked their way down the line of his jaw and then his neck once again, squeezing his dick. "Heck… How'd you get me into these…ah…situations?"

Maelgwn laughed, but the wolf didn't need to say more, nibbling and nipping at Alec's neck. His paw stroked that cock, squeezing around it lightly and adjusting the pressure of his fingers, sliding to the base and pushing the hare's underwear down a little further. The fur of his paw brushed that of the hare's crotch and he moaned with a lap of his lips, hunger rising inside him once again.

He had to have the hare and the feeling was very much mutual. Maelgwn checked Alec was not in risk of losing his balance as he adjusted his stance, needing to bend his knees a little more so he could grind his cock up against the hare's shaft. His length was a little longer and thicker – but size didn't really matter.

Alec moaned, his head spinning, need coursing through him. The hare rocked his hips, but he couldn't move all that much as Maelgwn held him in place, a sly grin pulling at the wolf's lips. Yet he would be well taken care of there, even though he wanted to glance around them once again, just to be sure they were alone. If they were going to be come upon, however, it would be far too late for either the wolf or the hare to do anything about it.

"Mmmph... Maelgwn..."

He moaned the wolf's name again, just to tease him. It was one of few things he could do in a situation like that, grunting as his shaft ground with a burst of pleasure up against the wolf's. Maelgwn groaned, rocking his hips, yet it was his large paw that wrapped around both his cock and the hare's, squeezing them together for greater friction.

Alec's ears twitched, yet he was lost to the wolf in nothing more than a breath of a moment. He panted heavily, trying to ease the tension in his lungs, but he just wanted to be there with his partner, lust coursing through him. His cock throbbed, yet it still felt so very small against the wolf's – in a good way. The slick flesh easing against him had him gasping for air and thrusting harder, yet it was clearly the wolf who was in control of the situation.

And he wouldn't have wanted it any other way at all. Not as Maelgwn thrust passionately against him, the knot slightly swollen at the base, but only so much so that the hare knew it was there. It would take a little more still, at the point of explosive climax, for it to grow fully, but it wouldn't be tied with the hare's rump that time. That was simply another treat of Maelgwn to enjoy later, straining Alec's backside deliciously wide around him.

The hare shivered, letting himself be lost there, for the wolf would always "find" him. If he was hunted, he was so very willing to be so, with the wind licking at his fur and the wolf's teeth sinking passionately into the juncture of his neck and shoulder. Alec gasped, though his head could not fall back when Maelgwn bit him as possessively as he did, teeth breaking skin in a couple of spots, though the flash of blood dancing on the wolf's tongue excited them both all the more.

"Mmmph... Yesss..."

The wolf let out a rasping, deep hiss into the hare's neck, fighting the urge to thrust with no holds barred. Yet he had to hold back, if only to squeeze and grind his dick against Alec's, letting the slickness of their pre-cum lube up the slide of their shafts just a little. The hare's member had a slenderer line to it than Maelgwn's, yet the wolf shuddered in pleasure, lust licking into his veins as heat seared through his body.

He was right where he needed to be, feeling the pull of shadows around him – and yet the wolf didn't want to be in any reality other than his own. As long as he got to be right there in that moment, with Alec, he would have forgone all the shadows and realities his mystical kind could ease into, for he wanted to ground himself there. Instead of feeling the world slip and ease around him, barely even ruffling his fur, he wriggled his toes, feeling the old stone of the bridge under his hind paws.

Maelgwn could not help but thrust harder and faster, keeping his strokes short, so as not to pull out too far before letting his need surge forward once again. He needed that contact, that friction, as if having their bodies connected in that way was all the wolf would need forevermore. The hare's body tightened deliciously against him and Maelgwn almost forgot to breathe for a moment, yet it was Alec grinding his cock against his that had him pressing on urgently, sensing that shift in desire swirling between them.

"Ah!"

Alec, however, was the first to pop as the wolf's knot swelled crudely against him. He knew what that meant and the surge of ecstasy rising within him demanded more still, exploding as seed surged from his shaft. Long, thin shots of cum pulsed from him, splattering over the wolf's paw and even the fur of their crotches, although neither would care about the mess.

Alec most certainly was not thinking about that as he leaned into Maelgwn, the wolf supporting him as his paw worked their shafts over.

The wolf bared his teeth in a growl, lapping over the spot on the hare's neck he'd bitten. Yet the pace of his paw on their dicks did not slow, spurred to a fever-pitch of desire as he rocked his hips, every fibre of his being howling at him to *thrust*.

Yet he had his hare and claimed him completely and utterly, helping him ride out his own orgasm even as he threw his head back and let loose a howl of climax. It echoed down the river and surely raised a few heads back in the village, but Maelgwn didn't have it in himself to care. Let them wonder who or what was howling out there, for he had all he needed right there in the moment. His lips rippled with a pleased snarl, thick, hot spurts of cum pouring over his paw, splattering up to Alec's lower abdomen and dripping down.

He gasped, breathlessly breaking his howl to laugh, struck by the sheer thrill of spending his load out there in the open. There could be no better way for a wolf to let loose their hunger and no better partner to do so with. Alec clung to him, his paws suddenly up on Maelgwn's shoulders, clinging to him as if for life itself.

With the wind wrapped around them, the cool of it bringing them down from their shared high and back to the present moment, they leaned into one another. Maelgwn's cock still dribbled cum as he captured Alec's lips in a hungry kiss, tongues tangling breathlessly, still longing for one another despite their recent orgasm.

There would be more to come, after hastily pulling their clothes back together, but both wolf and hare would find their lusts raised with the tease of risk clawing at their souls…

The Gwys Castle Cockatrice

The cockatrice sprawled out in the sunshine in the ruins of Castell Gwys, not caring if anyone happened upon him in his natural form. Of course, Gwern had learned how to take an anthro form over the years, but the cockatrice liked his feral one too, when it suited him. It was easier to get through life and engage with a more modern society (at least in his regarded opinion), when he could walk on two legs and upright, like an anthro with wing-arms for his rooster features.

He could, mostly, get away with pretending to be a rooster in anthro life, but his reptilian tail somewhat gave the game away. There were enough hybrids in the world that, if ever questioned, he could say his mother was a dragon and his father a rooster, although Gwern often wondered if anyone truly bought that story. Anthros mostly kept themselves away from him, sensing there was something innately "other" in the cockatrice, but Gwern had always been more at home when he was alone.

Gwern sighed lightly, dressed only in a loose pair of shorts that came down to his knees. His feathers were exposed to the sunshine, though they were a white and black shade, with spots slashed through them in a way he'd never seen in any other rooster. His green-grey tail curled out beautifully to his side, splashed across the grass, though there were feathers sprouting haphazardly from between the scales there too, with a curled, feathered tuft to the tip of it.

The castle had once been his home, many years ago. Time didn't have too much meaning to Gwen, the cockatrice living in the moment and focusing on more poignant events during his life.

Until, of course, Teilo had come along. The red fox had lived in Wales for most of his life but headed away for university and come back again from

England, travelling a little and getting to experience more of the world than Gwern. The cockatrice wondered just how that would be for him, one day, when he finally decided to move away from the little gamekeeper's cottage on the grounds of the castle, where he still had an agreement to live there. It was so archaic that it was a wonder he was even permitted residence, but Gwern was more than happy with a comfortable, small place to live, which hadn't changed in many years.

Yes, things had changed, most recently for the cockatrice. Gwen had not always been male, after all, but had once had breasts in his female form, though he had, for the time being, kept the pussy between his thighs. His form had been filled out, with a touch of magic, so he had broader shoulders and muscle in his chest and abs, stronger arms too. It was purely for his physical appearance, of course, for he didn't need to build muscle to demonstrate strength, which was innate to the cockatrice as a magical being.

But being as he was suited him. He could refer to himself as he liked, his identity shifting, though the one thing he did not have that mortals did was scars from removing his unneeded breasts on his chest. That was okay, however, as they could always be added in at some point if he wanted to allow his body to evolve further — but it felt more genuine to him to present himself as he felt in his heart and soul. It was Teilo who had taught him that, though it would take a while longer still for the cockatrice to even admit that to himself.

Still, he couldn't stay at the old castle forever as Teilo turned his attention to the wider world. There could be much more out there and his affiliation with the castle faded increasingly with every passing week. The castle was set on a hill, a more built-up motte and bailey castle that had been a point of interest in years gone by. When Gwern was not there, visitors came by to see the ruined stone walls, how they crumbled with the wear of the elements, yet the paths were well-maintained.

Hm… One day, I will come back to this castle just like that. Will I be a tourist too?

He wondered, tongue flicking out against his beak. Unlike that of a rooster, it was longer and more sinuous, like that of a reptile or a dragon, but it was not obvious unless he actually let it spill from his beak. Either way, it was certainly a part of his cockatrice body Gwern particularly liked and he shifted his weight from hip to hip, his dark hands back behind his head.

"Hey!"

Teilo bounded up to him, the red fox ever-present in bursts of energy that, frankly, left Gwern exhausted. Yet that was the way with energies like that moving around him, even though the transgender cockatrice wanted to see all he could do, all he was capable of – even if that meant he had to find a way to work with his natural way of being. More energy, working with the thrum of the earth and the world around him, would benefit Gwern in the long run.

"And hello to you too, Teilo."

He smiled at the fox, dressed in a loose T-shirt and similar, long shorts that suited the bright sunshine and the summer day, although there were clouds sweeping across the sky too that promised a break from the heat. Teilo offered him his paw, to help him up, although the cockatrice didn't really need it. He took it anyway, letting Teilo pull him up, the vulpine's lips parted in a typical, fox-ish grin.

Damn, that's infectious.

And so was Teilo's mood, the fox grabbing his hands without a second thought and pulling the cockatrice to him. However, pulling Gwern to him just appeared a little comical, since the cockatrice was head and shoulders taller than him, but they fit together all the same. Gwern wrapped his arms around the fox and drew him in tightly to him, his beak resting on top of Teilo's head, between his ears.

"You're cuter than you have any right to be," he murmured, his voice with a low rumble to it. "You know no one will bother us up here…"

"What?" Teilo barked a laugh and spun away, though the fox's eyes sparkled with mischief. "Gwern, we can't *always* do that out in the open! What if we really are caught?"

"Oh, but it's never happened before," Gwern countered. "Besides, it's my magic, the little twist of it, that keeps others away when I'm here, when we're together. You never have to worry about that."

Teilo cocked his head, ears flopping to the side. It was enough to make the cockatrice's heart beat quicker, feeling it resonate in his chest.

"But you have such a nice little cottage to go back to," he teased. "It's almost smaller than my student flat…"

"Hah!"

That startled a laugh from Gwern and the cockatrice swore he was falling for the fox all over again. He was quick of wit and made his heart skip beats that were really needed, but he loved Teilo for it, wanting to experience every moment with the fox he possibly could. His tail swung lightly back and forth and heat swelled within him, although he could have called halt to it if he wanted to.

But…Gwern simply didn't want to do anything about it. He just caught the fox's paw in his hand again and pulled him closer, a cloud sweeping over the sun to draw them into a cooling shade from its heat.

"It's a nice little place, but it could use some work," the cockatrice commented with a snarky, cheeky edge to his tone, though Teilo only laughed. "You might want to have a word with the landowner about that, you know."

"Oh, yeah?" Teilo grinned. "And what would the landowner say?"

"You'd have to tell me that. I mean," he said with a cheeky part of his beak, "you are a descendent of the estate owner nearest here… I forget the family name. I think the landowner is a pretty sly little fox who hangs around here to enjoy the company of a cockatrice. And that's why said cockatrice has not been kicked out of said cottage, so he can keep trying to get in his pants."

Teilo yelped and shook his head – but it was already clear to both of them it was more than accurate. The fox licked his lips, a little abashed, but he couldn't feel bad, not really. Not when Gwern was looking at him quite like that, like he was the cockatrice's whole world and then some, like the cockatrice wanted to throw him on the ground and ravish him right there and then.

I could see that happening…again.

The fox shivered as he was pushed back from the central grassy space in the castle – what remained of it, anyway. The cockatrice was strong and he allowed himself to be borne back with his back against the rough stone wall, marked with a little lichen and moss. It was a place he'd been in before, although he still splayed his ears a little shyly, shifting his weight from one hip to the other.

"Gwern…"

He blushed and licked his lips, but the cockatrice was there already, the rounded top of his beak brushing Teilo's upper lip gently. The moment was right and, even though he felt exposed, he let Gwern do with him as he willed, his lips parting to allow his tongue out in a lapping sweep against that of the cockatrice's.

Their kisses were different, yet still sensual, not able to lock lips even if they tilted their heads to opposite sides. Yet their kisses were a little wetter and messier, kissing with laps of their tongues up against one another, though Gwern sometimes deepened the kiss in his own sultry fashion by twisting his longer, more flexible tongue around and around Teilo's.

The cockatrice's lust surged in the kiss, pinning the fox passionately back against the stone wall, though he had no fear of it crumbling against them. His magic held it fast and the cockatrice leaned into his own power, wing-arms ruffling as his skin prickled with desire, tail sweeping back and forth.

Oh, how he needed him… Though, truthfully, either one of them could have had that thought, as if they were one and the same in the heat of the moment, passion soaring, demanding they give it due attention. Gwern growled into the fox's muzzle, pressing in close, though his hand roamed down the side of Teilo's body, finding a place to rest on his hip.

Just how the fox pushed in against him was alluring in itself, the cockatrice trying to take a full breath and finding need banded too tightly around his lungs for that. Gasping, Gwern broke the kiss and kiss-pecked his way down the fox's body, grabbing the hem of his shirt and helping the fox rip it up and over his head. Teilo obligingly raised his arms for the cockatrice, but his head was spinning too, the cool of the shade provided by the cloud cover not doing anything to ease the heat in his body.

With Gwern, it simply felt right, the cockatrice almost still grinding against him as he was liberated of his top. He didn't need it anymore, but Teilo couldn't stop himself from glancing around as his shirt was dropped aside, still checking for someone coming up the hill to the castle, someone who could have caught them in the act. Of course, the fox should just have trusted that Gwern's perception of them being safe was correct, as it was very true they hadn't been caught out there before.

Besides, it was kind of exhilarating to feel the fresh air caressing his fur, ruffling through it as if the wind itself was acting with a playful twist to it. He shivered as the cockatrice pulled his shorts down too, revealing his boxer briefs underwear, though they were already filling out with the swell of his shaft, aching for pleasure.

"Ohhh…"

He whimpered as Gwern teased the backs of his fingers, ever so slightly, across that bulge. The cockatrice was not rough with him in the slightest, but that mere touch had his cock throbbing, a drop of pre-cum marking his blue boxer briefs.

"You're wonderful like this," Gwern said in a low tone, as if something darker and more alluring still was winding through his form. "I can't wait to see all of you."

"Mm… Ah… What about you?"

"Oh, I'll not leave you wanting, don't you worry."

He was more concerned with pulling the fox's boxer briefs down first, peeling them down slowly from the waistband and pulling them over the bulging, growing member there. The fox's sheath folded down a little, tugging against Teilo's shaft, but his cock sprang free the moment Gwern allowed, a needy whimper breaking the fox's lips.

"Ohhh…"

"Perfect."

The cockatrice weaved slightly back and forth, shifting his weight from one foot to the other as if he was the one hypnotised. He pulled the fox's underwear down all the way and helped him step out of his shorts and his boxer briefs at once, revealing him in nothing but his natural, bare fur. A white slash of fur poured down his chest, though it tapered in the closer it grew to his crotch, until only a few, straggling white hairs marked his lower abdomen. Not all foxes were like that, though Gwern was rather partial to the white tip of his tail too, how he could see it flicking back and forth even from a distance.

"Mmm…"

Gwern crooned almost to himself as the fox's cock swelled, permitted such pleasure as the cockatrice's hand folded around it gently. The length thickened to its full size within his light grip, and he pumped the length a couple of times, letting Teilo grunt and groan against him, tongue lolling out from his muzzle.

"Ah… That… That feels…"

"Quiet, sweet," Gwern murmured, his eyes flicking up the fox's body to his muzzle and shining, pleading eyes. "Let me take care of you. You've done it for me so many times over."

His partner moaned and rocked his hips forward in non-verbal permission, though the cockatrice would never have pushed things if Teilo had given any indication at all, or explicitly said, that he was not okay with it. On the contrary, the whimpers and beautifully soft whines spilled from the fox's lips like wine: fine and coveted.

So, he leaned in a little, letting his beak nudge against either side of the fox's cock, tapered to a slender tip. The red length pulsed faintly under his touch and he let his long, sinuous tongue slip out, teasing to the base of Teilo's cock and dragging up. Yet he could do so much more with a tongue like that, curling around and slurping as drool spilled from his lips.

Teilo grunted and tipped his head back, baring the vulnerable expanse of his throat, head spinning. The clouds seemed to be moving above him and even the ground didn't seem as stable under his hind paws as it had before, heart pounding so vehemently that he felt it resonating through his chest with every thud. His lips parted and closed, over and over again, yet no words came out as that tongue curled and lashed pleasurably around his cock.

There was nothing quite like that tongue, the tip slender as it slapped around his cock in a lewd drip of saliva. A rush of blood shot straight into his length, throbbing deliciously, and he rolled his hips forward, soundlessly asking for more, always more. He wished he could pull words to his lips, yet it seemed more impossible than ever in a moment like that, when the only thing keeping him rooted in place was the cockatrice before him.

Gwern's tail swung back and forth as he licked up the length of that cock, enjoying the moment, though his own need rose. He did not yet have a cock to fill with blood and rise to attention, even if the cockatrice could if he really wanted one, but the folds between his thighs dampened with a slick of arousal. Squeezing his thighs together, he groaned in the back of his throat, though he would have been grinning from ear to ear if his beak had formed the draw of a smile.

He had more than enough ways to express himself, however, and ran a hand up the inside of the fox's leg, until he could gently cup his balls. His fingers closed around them, gently rolling and massaging Teilo's nuts between his fingers and thumb. It wasn't something that worked for every guy, as he had enjoyed a few relationships before Teilo, but it was one thing that had the fox's legs trembling, whimpering and practically melting into a puddle of lust right there before Gwern.

"Ah… Yes… Ohhhh!"

He grunted, tongue working as hard as it could within his muzzle to shape sounds into words, though there was no time that was more challenging than when the cockatrice was playing with his cock and balls. He swore he could *feel* the smirk in Gwern's eyes, as his beak could not do such, the sheer thrill of victory resounding through the cockatrice, just for being able to bring him to a panting, heaving pull of need like that.

The fox wiggled back and forth, shifting his hips from one side to the other, but he didn't want to escape the cockatrice, too locked into the moment to let anything slip away from him. His partner looked up at him, eyes glinting with need, and, slowly, rose.

"I promised you myself too, didn't I?"

The cockatrice's tail curled back and forth, showing off the flexibility of it as it moved more like a dragon's tail than any reptile that could surely be found in Wales, England or beyond. But Gwern wasn't thinking about that as he duly rid himself of his own shorts, eyes fixed on the fox's aching member. A bead of pre-cum clung to the tip where he had not had the heart to sweep it off and claim it for his own with his tongue, but he would have it in another way.

There was time enough for different kinds of passion and the moment was ripe for exactly what they needed as they renewed the connection between them once more. The fox groaned and dropped his eyes briefly to the folds between the cockatrice's thighs, already imagining the sweetness to be tasted there.

"Please… Can I taste you, first?"

Gwern blinked at him, though his beak parted in an easy smile, something deeper thrumming through him. Not lust but another four-letter word that, honestly, they needed to get around to saying. But saying it aloud meant so much more than they had come to so far and they were more than ready to let things move on, naturally, like the flow of a river curling and dipping around them.

"Yes…"

His heart swelled. The fox really accepted him as he was – and that was something Gwern was sure no other partner had done for him, not fully, not quite. His tail curled and he stepped in impulsively to flick his tongue out to Teilo's in a passionate, wet kiss.

They moaned into it, drifting away for a while, but Teilo's throbbing need was not to be set aside so easily. Even as their cries mingled in the kiss, grunts and soft, damp moans, the cockatrice's hand found the fox's cock again, closing around it to lightly stroke up and down. He didn't want Teilo to lose control too swiftly, after all, for there was only one place he could go that day.

However, he broke the kiss with panting delight, a splash of sunshine falling over them only briefly as a cloud moved away from the sun. They dipped deeper into the ruins where there was a low wall at the right height for Gwern to lean on, even if they would spend time cuddling in Gwern's bed too later that day. As much as Teilo teased that they should be more civilised and spend time indoors when they were naked, the fox was just as daring as Gwern was, chasing down desire as if he was on the hunt.

As the cockatrice leaned over and flicked up his tail to expose his tight rump and the gleam of arousal marking his pussy, the fox eagerly dropped to his knees. Oh, of course: it would only be a taste. His cock was too hard, throbbing anxiously, for him to bring the cockatrice off like that too, but Gwern wanted to be filled.

His tongue swiped eagerly up along the cockatrice's pussy, following his slit from the clit to the patch of flesh between his pussy and anal pucker. Yet he could not resist delving between them to lap up deeply into Gwern's sweet heat, scooping his liquid arousal out so he could drink down the aphrodisiac. He moaned against the cockatrice's pussy, grabbing his hips to help him grind back on to his muzzle, tongue lapping and curling, dragging over his clit as it swelled lightly, more obvious with the cockatrice's folds parted lightly.

"Ah… Ohhh, that's good," Gwern moaned. "But…I need you too, inside me, deep inside."

"Mmm, soon…"

The fox took his time to steal a few more laps, slurping lewdly up with a wet slap of his tongue. He didn't want to mount his partner without the taste of the cockatrice on his lips and in his muzzle, greedily swallowing every drop of arousal he could. He wanted it, pupils dilating a little as lust got the better of him, his cock throbbing crudely, wanting to plunge it deep in the cockatrice.

But it was what they both craved so very intimately, so he rose with his cock in his paw, presenting the tip of it to Gwern's slick, wet pussy. He pressed inside slowly, making sure his cock slid deep, though the cockatrice's body hugged him tightly like he was made to be inside them. The natural wetness of his arousal made it much easier to push inside his cunny than his ass, although both pleasures were wonderful in different ways.

Gwern cried out with a hoarse groan, his entire body shaking until the heated rod of the fox was buried fully inside him. Was there anything as good as being filled and penetrated just like that? The fox's cock had always fit him so well, but Gwern had a sly suspicion in the back of his mind that it was the deeper intimacy and connection between them that made sex as spectacular as it was.

Ah, it was something he would think about later, preferring to sink into the moment, the feel of the fox's paws on his hips, stroking up his feathers. Wrapping his tail around the fox's midsection, he tightened his grip, letting the vulpine know in no uncertain terms that he was ready for more.

Teilo followed his lead with thrust after thrust, hugging his arms around the cockatrice's body and letting him bear their weight. He had no concerns at all that Gwern would not hold them up as he was, need trembling through as passion rose. The cockatrice's pussy gripped him tightly, a warm, wet glove that pulled along the length of his cock, and he moaned aloud, his strokes speeding up.

It was right where he needed to be with the shadow of the ruins falling over them, splashing them in a cool lilt. He moaned and ducked his head, pressing it against the cockatrice's back, though he was not tall enough, with the small height difference between them, to push his chin over Gwern's shoulder. His cock powered deep, aching as if the knot was going to swell at the base, though it was still squishy and mostly unformed. He would lock with the cockatrice when the time was right – or perhaps that was best for a long, slow session back in Gwern's cottage.

Teilo groaned, tongue lolling from his mouth as he lapped without thinking against the cockatrice's upper back, pulling the appendage over his feathers. Gwern shuddered against him, but he thrust harder, following his partner's lead as he powered into him.

Desire twisted and curled around them: a tangible force they needed so very desperately. The fox's hips bounced lightly off Gwern's ass with every thrust, letting the cockatrice push back at him to tell him just how hard he could go. The tightness of that tail clutching him wasn't going to release its grip in the slightest unless he spent his load inside the cockatrice – and he had every intention of doing so.

Gwern moaned as he was filled, arms trembling, though his fingers gripped the stone of the wall firmly, the rounded, worn stones jutting up from the top of it. It was not the kind of wall that would have been at all comfortable to sit on, yet the dark stone was comforting and reassuring in its own way. He squeezed around the shaft filling him, almost loathe to let the fox pull back in any way at all. Yet that pull of tension at his core wound itself tighter and tighter, letting him know just how close he was to climaxing. Bracing his legs, he did his best to spread them apart a little more, but it didn't really matter in the heat of a moment like that.

One way or another, they would have their fill of each other, panting and heaving, letting what was to come between them flow.

The fox thrust harder, his knot growing, grinding against the folds of the cockatrice's sex – but he didn't push in. No, he'd decided that was for later, even as an aching, primal need snarled through him, demanding he knot his partner and seal the deal. That could be replicated, by the clutch of a well-timed paw and he near enough held his breath as he speared deep and relished in the clenching pull of silken sweetness around his cock.

In the end, he squeezed his knot, hard, at just the right moment, for neither fox nor cockatrice could be sure which of them climaxed first. One moment, Teilo was still thrusting and the next the cockatrice was scrabbling at the wall for support, rolling bliss sweeping through him. A stray feather drifted away, to be forgotten in the grass, and the fox tried to keep his cock buried as deep as it would go, rocking and juddering his hips up to Gwern's ass.

Long shots of virile fox seed splattered into him and the cockatrice pulled his tail securely around Teilo as the unleashed his lust, panting heavily through waves of ecstasy. It was hard to retain control of one's senses when it came to a point of bliss like that, yet Gwern's orgasm rippled and pulled, however erratically, around the fox's cock, milking him, even then, of every lustful drop he possibly had to give.

The fox's climax tapered off first, but he was loathe to pull out, wanting to stay inside the cockatrice despite his cock, slowly, softening. Gwern keened softy as it tugged free, a spill of cum marking his folds in its wake, though he quivered and half-turned his head as if to rest his beak against Teilo's muzzle.

"You feel so good inside me, with me," he whispered, barely raising his voice. "Will you…stay home with me tonight? I have dinner, beef… And that card game you liked."

Teilo chuckled and nuzzled the cockatrice's back, even if he was still a little light-headed. He stood up, keeping a paw on Gwern's hip as he helped his partner stand again too.

"You went into town for me?" He teased, nuzzling into the cockatrice's chest as Gwern's arms went back around him, where they belonged. "Not just for work?"

"Mmm, just for you."

The fox's heart warmed and he blushed, though it was the wrong moment for his shyness to demand attention back in the forefront of his mind. It was okay, however, and he took the cockatrice's hand as they stepped apart again – but not too far apart.

"Then…let's do it."

Together, they had much more to explore, redressing in just their shorts and heading down to the cottage on the edge of the old grounds of the castle, where no one would bother them. Truthfully, Gwern even had issues getting post and packages delivered there, his natural powers helping others evade him, as always. But it was a price he was willing to pay for his life as it was – only, the fox had been far too persistent for his kind of magic to work on Teilo.

The cockatrice would forever be glad of that, all so he could have what he had with the vulpine. Hopefully, always and forever.

That story, however, was to be told all in their own time.

The Maiden & the Afanc

Lily exhaled as she stood on the banks of Llyn Barfog, the lake stretching out before her. The golden-furred husky curled her bare toes into the grass, the land around her rich and luscious on the cusp of summer, though it still felt like spring had a blossoming hold on the land of legends. It had been some time indeed since the canine anthro had returned to the lake to see about meeting up with "Afanc" again, but she'd had her university studies, down in Cardiff, to bear in mind, of course.

Afanc… Well, she didn't really know his name, which was probably a bad thing, but he'd never been unkind to her, no. It had to be a nickname. In Welsh, "afanc" meant "monster" – specifically the monster that, supposedly, had been dragged into Barfog lake, if one believed the myth. It was no secret, obviously, as to why her friend had chosen that name for himself as he rather looked like the supposed monster.

Just an anthro… Rather than the creature in the story she'd read and re-read, trying to make sense of him and the mystery Afanc held in him. He stood tall, easily over six-and-a-half feet in height, with a dragon-like face. It was not fully reptilian, however, but had a cap of brown, beaver-like fur over the crown of his head, between what could have been short, gnarled horns or a feature of his face. It was hard to say, though his kind smile more than made up for what could have been quite an intimidating look otherwise.

His body, unlike his dragon-like head, was furred like a beaver – and the reference to that species clearly came through in the flat splay of his tail. Regardless of what secrets Afanc did or did not keep, it was clear he was a hybrid of some kind, not belonging to any one type of anthro. Hybrids had become moderately common, enough so that seeing one was not a surprise, but he seemed like an odder kind of mismatch, body parts not quite coming together seamlessly.

Maybe he'd been teased for looking "weird" when he was younger, but he'd not let on when she'd asked him about that, regardless of all the summers and holidays she'd spent up at the lake, visiting family nearby. She felt she knew him well – and yet not at all at the same time. With his thick, beaver-like tail, he was quite a good swimmer, his body well-muscled overall, even if his fur hid some of that definition from view. Some may have described his appearance as "shaggy," but Lily would not have been so unkind.

He was supposed to meet her out there, on the edge of the lake with the mountains rising behind, but he was late, as always. That was Afanc's "move," if she could call it that, though she half-turned with a smile on her lips as the breeze ghosted her long, blonde hair against the back of her neck.

"Shwmae, Afanc," she said, grinning more widely as she turned to face him, looking like he always had and that cheeky smile pulling at his lips. "You're late."

"No, no," he said, closing the distance between them as he hugged her, his arms going around her, though his hands seemed somewhat scalier than before with big, chunky crocodile-like skin. "I'm exactly when I said I'd be here!"

She scoffed and rolled her eyes, gesturing at the sun.

"It's going to be night soon! You know how quickly it gets dark around here when the sun dips behind the mountains. Or you should know better than me, Afanc: you're the one who lives here."

He grinned and shook his head, taking a step back as he took her paws in his large hands. Against herself, Lily blushed. Why was her heart suddenly pounding so hard?

"Ah… Here, I brought your book back, both of them."

She fumbled in her bag for something to do, even though she didn't really need to give Afanc's books back right away. He was the same as he'd been for the last three years she'd hung out with him and yet she felt a draw to him, like something had changed between them in the slow spill of crimson sunset across the lake.

He stilled her, a gentle hand on her wrist. Lily sucked in a breath, the dog's tail lifting a little. What was wrong with her? Something was different. *Something* had *shifted*.

She looked him in the face, taking a breath, though it did nothing to steady her. He was ruggedly handsome, to her, and she splayed her ears, blushing as she looked away.

"Lily, you know I only come out here for you, right?"

She blinked at him.

"Here? Me?"

He nodded gently, his smile softening, though his brown eyes shone with sincerity.

"I've been hidden away for too long, Lily," he said. "I say I've been studying, that I'm doing a research project for a grant… Well, I have and I am, but that's not the point of why I'm out here on my own, practically. I've been doing those things, but I never feel as present and as *solid* as I do when I'm with you, Lily. Things with you… They're different. They always have been. But it gets lonely out here, every time you leave."

Her lips twisted in sympathy.

"Oh, Afanc… I didn't know you felt that way," she breathed. "I… Why do you stay out here, if you're all on your own? I know you've said there's few around here and I get that, but you don't have to stay here. You could move to England, head down to the south coast – even over to the west coast of Wales too. There's more for you to do, more you can do to find yourself, Afanc."

His smile widened, though there was a sheen of shyness in his eyes.

"With you, Lily, I *am* myself. Only with you. And…I hope you feel the same. This is forward, but that's the way I am – and you're the only one who's ever accepted me the way I am."

She swallowed hard, blinking away light tears. Emotion surged in her chest and her lips trembled into a smile, relief flooding her.

Oh, thank goodness.

To have her feelings returned was all she ever could have asked for. Her heart tried to leap and juddered in her chest, suddenly feeling shakier than she honestly had any right to be. Lily tried to take a step back, but he caught her gently by her elbows, stopping her from going too far away from him. She was more than content, however, to stay where he wanted her, as if an invisible cord connected her to Afanc, forever linking them. Lily would have thought that marvellously romantic at another time, but, well…was it really so bad? Was it really all so farfetched?

No… No. Not at all. But she had to know, had to be sure.

"Afanc, you're talking in a way that could mean several different things at once," she said a little shakily, gently disengaging her elbows from his grasp. "This isn't fair to me, if you muddy the waters."

Afanc laughed lightly, yet there was something of the rippling music of the lake water in his tone. She loved that, heart skipping a beat, even if it was not a sound the husky had ever heard replicated anywhere else. Like so many little notes, it was something unique to Afanc.

"I don't mean to do that, Lily, trust me," he said. "But I… This is hard to get out. This is my home, this is where I belong. I can't just leave the lake."

He looked at her with such an earnest look in his eyes that she believed him, even if Lily could not say she understood him fully, not in the slightest. It didn't make sense that he couldn't just leave, for she had never seen him with any form of family – or, indeed, any other friends for that matter too. Yet Afanc must have had them, some, any, even if she suddenly felt that prying into that side of Afanc's life may have been too nosy, upturning stones that she had no right to look under.

"I think… I think, I understand," she said softly, her eyes casting over the sweep of the mountains, shadows slowly darkening the slopes as the sun sank behind them. "It's just… I want you to be happy too, Afanc. I'm out here, going away and coming back, but you're here. I love that you're a constant here, someone who *belongs*, but…I don't know. I keep coming back and it feels like another home to me now. Even if I don't have a real home elsewhere…"

"Then stay here, with me," he offered, extending his hand to her. "We can get you a place in town…if you don't want to stay with me. I'd never force anything, but the offer is there."

Lily smiled and looked away, a giggle bubbling up from her lips.

"What? Here? I… I…"

She wanted to say that she couldn't possibly, that it was madness speaking, and yet…it made sense. It was somewhere she had returned to, time after time again, coming home to the peaks and valleys that felt like they were cradling her, welcoming her home as they carved stark lines across any horizon.

Hiraeth.

It meant so much more than what the word had become twisted to mean in pop culture, but that wasn't something Lily honestly wanted to let her mind linger on in that moment. It didn't belong there, but the sense of *belonging* in the mountains did, that innate feeling of coming home, of having somewhere that was absolutely meant for her above all else.

She took a deep breath, filling her lungs with crisp mountain air, the lightness of the lake flitting across her tongue. It was funny how even that could be tasted, her sense of smell playing as much a part in that as ever. Afanc allowed her space to work through her own thoughts, her emotions, and a wave of gratitude swept through her.

"I've been looking for somewhere that's mine for these years," she murmured, "but going from place to place… That's not me."

"You'll still want to travel though, Lily, I'm sure."

Was it wrong for her to like how her name sounded on his lips so much, as if his slenderer tongue was curling sensually around it even as it broke from his mouth? Lily's eyes lingered on his lips for longer than was polite before she shook herself out of it. She hoped Afanc had not noticed and yet the husky found herself not caring too much anyway.

The veil at the lake was thin and she yearned to break through it, a sensation of something pulling in her chest. Tipping her chin up, as if in defiance of something she could not see, the husky stepped boldly forward and rested a paw on his biceps. With what Afanc was wearing, a short-sleeved T-shirt, she curled her fingers around the muscle lightly, unable to catch herself in time to stop herself from rubbing her fingers back and forth.

"Of course," she said. "But maybe you can come with me."

His eyes lit up and Afanc's beaver-like tail twitched.

"Really? You would take me with you?"

"Not in chains, Afanc," she laughed, pulling away from him, but only in light-hearted mirth. "But if you want to come…yes. Before then, I think we have much to work out between us."

"Yes."

One word was all it took as he stepped in and closed the distance between them. Afanc tipped Lily's chin up once more, lips so close to hers, but paused, searching her eyes. The husky's heart leapt in her chest and she let out an involuntary whimper, breath hitching in her throat, though she made no move to pull away. On the contrary, that moment was all they needed to say all that their words were not quite ready to, the canine making the first move to press her lips to his.

Her ears splayed and her tail lifted lightly, wagging as he deepened the kiss with a moan that was almost throaty, deeper and resounding through her. Lily could not help but respond in kind as her blood sang for him, heat racing under the fragile surface of her skin, her fur doing nothing to help protect her from the vulnerability Afanc unleashed in her. Yet it was a good kind of vulnerability, to be that open with someone she trusted so completely and utterly, so she would speak no ill of it, letting her body sink into the moment and move with the flow of it.

She'd spent so long resisting the river rushing downstream through life, after all, that she'd forgotten to let the rhythms of life take her sometimes too. And maybe that was just one of many reasons she'd been drawn back to Llyn Barfog over and over again to rest and rejuvenate, finding it one of few places in the country where she felt like herself.

Perhaps, with Afanc, she was truly home too, truly herself.

The kiss broke faintly, their lips parted, chests heaving. Instantly, Lily wanted to close the fragile distance between them, strengthening the connection she had only just uncovered. If that would be so wrong then the husky never again wanted to be right.

"Ah… Lily…"

His voice was huskier and rougher than before and that made her hungrier for him, blushing at the desire flowing through her body. Her fingers curled, leaning into him as she leaned her head on his chest, one ear pricked to listen to the similarly frantic pounding of his heart.

"Are you stopping me?" She challenged. "I might have to take another of your books away if so, just to make sure you invite me back again."

Afanc laughed, relief oddly rolling through his tone. That was something Lily would ask him about later, of course, but it would have to wait just a little while longer. As increasing darkness spilled down the slopes of the mountains, like the patient shadows were swallowing the land with the lure of nightfall, Afanc tugged her gently along with him, taking her paw in his.

"Let's go somewhere quieter, along the lake."

There was no one around there, but Lily liked the feel of her paw in his, fingers slotting easily between his. Could the two of them really been made to fit one another or was that just her making more of the moment than what it was? Ah, but love or even connection was so rare those days that the husky clung tenaciously on to it, unwilling to release it even a fraction until she had played out every last second of what their moments had to offer them.

Thankfully for Lily, those moments were to be many years together and not mere minutes or seconds. The husky was simply not to know that at the time, the chains that had held Afanc back falling away, link by link, as another finally opened their heart to him.

He led her around the edge of the lake where it curved and offered a slight ridge and place to sit, though the grass swelled with luscious green and not the deeper hues that came in late summer and autumn. She shivered lightly, wrapping her arms around her torso, yet the chill was fleeting. It was hard not to feel warm, shifting her weight from one hind paw to the other, when Afanc's eyes were on her, seeing more to the husky than Lily was sure she even saw in herself.

They were not far from civilisation but far enough away that there didn't seem to be any stray walkers around them, no one exploring the lake that evening. That was strange enough in itself, but Lily didn't care as she met Afanc's eyes once again, finding herself reflected in them. Or perhaps not herself, per se, but her need – the want to be close in a way they never had before.

Goodness, what is wrong with me? She could have laughed with herself, how forward she was being – and yet it didn't feel wrong in the slightest. *I couldn't even wait to get back to my rental cottage, or his place?*

The answer to that was resolutely "no" as he reached for her and she went gladly into his arms, ignoring the driving beat of her heart in her chest. It had no business pounding on her ribcage in such a frantic manner, delicious heat pooling in her lower abdomen, making her want to press her thighs together. She belatedly regretted wearing as much as she had to meet Afanc, but Lily could not have envisioned the turn their evening together would have taken, regardless of how glad she was for it.

His thumb gently caressed her lower lip and the husky instinctively lapped against it, sweeping the flexible, pink appendage against his thumb in a quick, sweeping motion. Afanc groaned subtly and she smirked, unable to help just how she adored the effect she had on him. Even if she felt she was falling too quickly, he was right there with her.

"No one is going to bother us here."

Something in his tone told her he was serious, that Afanc truly meant it, and her heart leapt. She caressed his face again and kissed him deeply, their lips somehow fitting together perfectly despite the different shapes of their muzzles.

"Oh…"

Lily moaned softly into his touch, though she would have been lying if she wanted to say she'd never thought about kissing him before that day. She'd just thought that wasn't what their relationship was like, that the hybrid anthro…well… She'd never asked him upfront how he felt about her and perhaps that was something she should have been clearer about too.

So, Lily melted into Afanc's touch as if her body was meant to meld to the shape of his, his broad chest holding her firmly as his arm encircled her waist passionately. His fingers cupped the curve of her waist and she shivered, as if a fire had been lit under her skin. Afanc's free paw came up and stroked the line of her jaw gently, tenderly, as if he was trying to take great care with her.

She explored his mouth lightly with her tongue as their lips parted to deepen the kiss further, both knowing exactly where things were going as their bodies arched into one another. Lily caught her breath, nostrils flaring ever so slightly as she was forced to breathe through her nose, though it grounding her having Afanc there with her, stride for stride and paw in paw. His tongue curled against hers and she let out a needy, blissfully trembling moan as it flicked over hers, tempting her to lean into him even more than she already was. Alas, Lily could not be swallowed by his body, as much as Afanc supported her weight, holding her tightly and closely.

Breaking the kiss, the husky moaned softly, so quietly that it could have been merely a breath.

"I am *not* that easy to break," she murmured, surprising even herself with her husky tone. "Is this what you brought me out here to say, to do?"

It was Afanc's turn to blush, though the fur of his muzzle mostly kept it hidden from view. The only "tell" was his fingers tightening their grip on her waist.

"I hoped… I hoped you would feel the same as I do," he confessed, eyes bright, almost shiny with emotion. "But I didn't know, not this… I didn't know how you would truly feel, if it would change anything."

She kissed him again, her lips following the line of his scaled jaw as he grunted. It was gratifying to catch Afanc by surprise at last and she kiss the crook of his neck as he tipped his head back slowly but obligingly for her. Her lips found his Adam's apple, tenderly brushing over it, but she could not have Afanc in his clothes for much longer.

"I want you, to find out what this is between us," she said clearly, a smile dancing over her lips. "Do you? Is this what you want?"

"Oh, heavens, *yes*."

He kissed her passionately and her mind blurred, as if the present moment contained enough joy in it for a thousand moments all at once to collide. Their paws moved more urgently against one another, though they were in sync, pulling at T-shirts as he raised his arms over his head to let Lily bare his torso to the cool evening air. She was quick to follow as he helped her out of her own, revealing more of her golden fur and the white that dipped between her breasts to his ravenous eyes.

Yet they could barely bear to bring themselves to break from the kiss as they determinedly undressed one another, stripping each other down and tumbling to the grassy mound. Lily laughed, force to lose his lips for a moment, as he tugged at her jeans, getting the button undone and then requiring her help to get her out of them. With her head spinning, the husky did what she could to assist, kicking off her custom paw-shoes and lifting her hips so he could get her jeans down. They pulled her panties along with them, leaving her lower half swiftly bare.

A tingle of exposure pulled at her and she blushed, half-turning her muzzle away, even if it was not a moment in which for any manner of embarrassment to claw its way into her soul. Not when she could be there to savour and relish in every second, watching him unbuckle his synthetic belt and, slowly, slide his jeans down. Somehow, she was on her knees and he was standing, though the husky could not have been entirely sure when the two of them had switched positions. It was not something that mattered in the heat of a connection like that, gently, helping him get them down and off his hind paws, which were large and dragon-like – in keeping with his hybrid form.

She didn't know what to expect as she looked up at him and Afanc trembled, turning his muzzle away. All that remained on their bodies was his underwear and, of course, her bra, which they had not yet got around to removing.

"It's okay," she said gently, kneeling there, her fingers toying with the hem of his underwear, the loose boxers offering a thicker rise in front than she may have expected. "I accept you as you are, Afanc. And we don't have to go any further if you don't want it."

His chest juddered as he took a deep breath that didn't appear to have come easily at all.

"It only frightens me just how much I *do* want it, Lily, how much I want you and only you."

Her head rang with that, warmth curling around her core as if it was settling there, showing her what she had been missing in life, all the times when she could have been with Afanc but was in other parts of the country. Lily pressed a gentle kiss to his stomach, the beaver-fur a little coarser than what she was used to, but she loved it all the same. Just wanting to know every part of Afanc had her pressing in close with a needy whimper, shuddering against him.

She couldn't stop herself from sliding his underwear down, but the prize inside was not to be anticipated. For not one shaft but two sprang free, his sheath housing both, and the husky gasped aloud.

"Oh, wow… I don't think you'll fit both at once!"

He laughed along with her and the husky helped him out of his undergarments, though they thankfully didn't hook around his tail, which helped somewhat. But she was more than merely interested in his shafts, how they appeared ridged with a spiralling rise turning around and around each of them. The lower one was a little smaller, but they were a good size for her, without being too intimidating.

She played her paw up the length of the uppermost one, letting her fingers ease around the ridges as she explored him, vaguely taking note of his heavy balls too, large and full. Those were impressive, she had to admit, and Lily could only imagine, for the time being, just how his seed would feel spurting inside her, filling her up. There had to be an awful lot stored up in there.

"Oh…"

Afanc moaned lightly and rocked into her touch, the world around them growing a little darker again, for twilight fell swiftly in the mountains. Lily chuckled and worked out how to close her fingers around his cock, though the ridges, in that instance, did get in the way. She'd work it out, however, feeling how the ridges compressed under her fingers, allowing some measure of pliability. She squirmed. How would they feel slipping inside her? Even though her lower body was completely bare, she was sure she was already wet, though her legs were slightly parted. A light breeze tickled her folds and she grunted, pressing in closer to Afanc so she could explore him.

"I've never seen a dick like yours," she admitted, tail wagging. "But I want to know every part of you, Afanc."

"That's crude for you," he commented lightly, though it was only a gentle tease. "I want to know every part of you too, Lily. I want…everything, every part of you. I feel guilty just standing here while you're…mmph."

He groaned as she licked the head of his uppermost member, taking advantage of the moment as she explored him. Lily moaned and pressed down, parting her lips to take his shaft experimentally into her mouth, her soft tongue caressing his ridges and bobbing her muzzle along the full length. It was easy enough to take with the shape of her muzzle, but the husky took her time, wanting to enjoy it. It was not often in life she felt she could slow down and truly experience things.

Well, that was the case when she was with Afanc and maybe that was just one more reason why they were always meant to be together, forever and always. She couldn't say completely how she knew that in her heart, but it felt right. That was all it needed to be, no more than that. Yet it was everything at the same time.

She sucked on his cock, experimenting with different caresses of her lips and moaning once more to let the subtle vibrations from her lips travel into his cock too. Her paw came up to stroke his other shaft, reminding herself she had to please both of them at once, or at least try to give them somewhat even attention. Lily flicked her tongue temptingly around the base of his cock and dragged it up, bobbing her head as she got into the motion.

Afanc stroked her head, behind her ears, and she pressed on, sucking and slurping around him, ignoring the gleam of saliva around her lips. It didn't matter that there was something of a mess there, not when her heart was pounding as hard as it was, but she wanted to know him, truly. Her paw wandered to his balls, stroking around them and feeling their weight, but that was a part of Afanc she would have to take time to learn his sweet spots. With Lily's paw more easily cupping around to his ass, she gave his rump a wicked squeeze, her fingers digging into briefly as she took what she thought was rightfully hers.

"Unff... Lily!"

He tried to stop her, but the husky pressed on for a few more moments, her ears splayed as she bobbed on his cock, trying to nuzzle all the way down to his crotch every time she sank deeply. She just wanted to take as much of him into her mouth as possible, lips folding softly and sensually around his ridges, losing herself.

Lily, however, pulled back as he asked, his fingers brushing insistently around her ears. The husky wagged and looked up at him, resisting the urge to rest her chin on his hip, for Afanc was already in motion.

He drew the canine with him gently as he sat back on the little rise of the grass, the mound allowing him to sit a little more with his torso at an angle. Afanc caressed her hips as he gently brought her over him, straddling his waist. The husky tried to sink, but it was harder to angle herself when she had two shafts to deal with rather than just the one. Idly, Lily wondered just how it could feel to have him gently stretching out both her pussy and her tail hole at once, but she wasn't immediately all that adventurous. In time, she would surely get that experience for herself too.

Afanc blinked up at her as he gently took his shaft in his paw and angled it for her, pointing it up at her pussy as she sank slowly on to him. It took a couple of attempts to get everything just as it needed to be, tipping her torso forward towards him a little, a paw resting on his chest with her fingers splayed. His heart beat strongly, sending a pumping beat into her paw, travelling up her arm.

"Ah…"

She exhaled as he slowly stretched her out with just one shaft – and the husky found herself more than wet enough to take him completely into her, considering that they took it slowly and patiently. Between them, there was no rush, though Lily still tasted Afanc on her tongue, lapping gently around her muzzle as she savoured every drop, every throb of his essence slipping up inside her.

"Lily… You're beautiful…"

She blushed, meeting his eyes. With the light fading, it was difficult to pick out all the subtleties of his features, but she had mapped them all in her memory anyway. She wanted to kiss over every inch of his reptilian muzzle and stroke around the backs of his horns, fingers sliding naturally down to the back of his neck so she could stretch up and kiss him deeply all over again. The husky moaned, rocking her hips, riding him even as Afanc planted his dragon-like feet into the softer ground, gaining leverage to rock up into her.

"Oh!"

Lily groaned, her entire body trembling as they came together. It was more than she needed, so much more in the heat of the moment, her skin prickling and tingling with desire that simply could not be kept in for a single second longer. She panted heavily, her pink tongue spilling out, though she rested her other paw on his shoulder, curling her fingers around almost possessively. Holding on to Afanc helped ground her in the moment, her pussy tightening reflexively around his shaft, though she couldn't grip him rhythmically or really all that deliberately at all.

But she could rise and fall more swiftly, luxuriating in the feel of being so perfectly full, her folds hugging his shaft as she rode him. Afanc's paw held on to her hip, thumb rubbing in slow, gentle circles, though he bucked up readily into her, matching her lust stroke for stroke. His second shaft slipped against her ass, pushed down where it was not needed at that time, though his sheath had at least enough suppleness in it to allow that flexibility. Still, it had to be additional stimulation for Afanc too as his nostrils twitched, puckering with needy grabs at breath that did not fully sate him.

Yet the husky would be more than enough to satisfy his heart in every way. She moaned and rode him more urgently, her hips falling more quickly with every bounce of her buttocks on him. Her tail lifted where it had no real need to, though Lily didn't care. She ground down passionately on his second shaft, only holding back enough to make sure she was not so rough with Afanc that she didn't bend his cock crudely. It would have been too much, of course, but Afanc didn't seem at all put out by anything she did on top of him.

Afanc groaned under her as she squeezed around him, clenching with her pussy again and again, though her arousal flowed freely, slick where their bodies joined. She bore down hard enough that she felt his sheath crumple back lightly, using every inch of shaft he had for her, their moans rising in desperation.

It was a good thing Afanc could keep others away from them while they were enjoying one another – but that was yet another little thing Lily would not learn about him until later. There were still sweet revelations to come to light, though only things that would bring them closer together than ever, learning every last little thing about one another to know the other as their partner, completely and utterly.

Lily whimpered on top of him, her body feeling close to the edge, but Afanc was a sweet enough lover to slide his paw to the front of her pussy, fingertips finding her clit. She thrust with raw want and need on top of his cock, her body torn between grinding forward into his hand and arching back and down on to his cock. All in all, it was a wonderful conundrum to be in and she drifted, letting him take greater control as he thrust up passionately into her.

The pressure on her clit was just right, rubbing back and forth as a jolt of pleasure lanced inside her. She moaned his name, though could not even be sure it was coherent as she rode him, barely even managing to move her hips as Afanc thrust lustfully up into her, bringing her hips down lightly to meet him each time. His breath caught and yet his eyes never once left hers, as if he had captured her in that moment and, one way or the other, simply refused to let her go.

Together, they rocked closer to climax, but Afanc must have been holding back until she hit her high. Lily moaned and curled forward towards him, rounding her shoulders, but she was helpless to do anything other than grind on to him passionately as orgasm claimed her in a pull of ecstasy. The canine moaned through climax as Afanc trembled and bucked up against her, his claws raking through the loamy soil as he filled her with every inch of his length.

Moments after she tensed on his cock, her pussy rippling and pulling around him, though the husky was hardly in control of that, he hit his high too. And she got to adore every tangible moment, like how his head twisted to the side and Afanc let out an almost strangled roar. His cock felt larger than ever, seed flowing deep inside her with spurt after thick spurt, though not all of it could stay in her pussy as it leaked back out from the join of their bodies.

His second cock, of course, could not be spared the ejaculation too, though the seed mostly missed her, only a few wild splatters catching the underside of her tail and buttocks. Most landed on his thighs and marked his own hide, though there would be a dip in the lake for them to wash off soon enough. A little mess really was by the by.

She moaned, letting it all roll over her, through her, languishing in the moment. It was a moment she wished she could stay in forever, experiencing all it had to give her, chest heaving, still wearing her bra. But she'd feel his paws on every inch of her body in due course. Out there, with the mountain breeze licking at her fur and dancing around her ears, she was already right where she needed to be, lustfully impaled on his shaft.

Eventually, however, each long, lustful spurt of seed had to slow and come to a halt, the husky left heaving and panting over him, tongue still lolling passionately from her muzzle. Lily sank slowly to his chest and he wrapped his arms around her, his cock slowly softening inside her pussy as they came down from their respective highs.

Afanc caressed her muzzle gently and she tucked her nose into the crook of his neck. Soon, they would move back to his place, which was hardly any distance at all from the lake, and wonder at how they'd taken their first time with each other out there, in the open, like it was the most natural thing in the world. Yet it was right for the maiden and the afanc, despite Afanc's history remaining to be told, filling in the dark corners of his past with glorious light and hope, all by Lily's paw.

Together, they had a whole life together to explore.

They couldn't wait to get started.

Seduction of a Sea Serpent

Nia took a breath of fresh, ocean air as she turned her face to the sea, though she wasn't heading down into the estuary that day. Even though that was typically where Osien was to be found, with the name he had most recently chosen for himself, the sea serpent mostly kept himself to himself. The estuary was too busy those days and there were still gift shops and the like selling trinkets of Barmouth's "sea serpent," drawing attention to the oceanic dragon-creature when all Osien had ever wanted was to live his life in peace.

Heather on the cliff grew ruggedly, in yellow and purple, yet it was not as prosperous as it could have been. There were tourists and locals hiking more than ever and Nia was not so sure that was a good thing for Osien. Of course, the stoat wanted to see more anthros, just like herself, heading out into the wilds of the world, but there were some parts of the wilderness that were best left undisturbed.

She didn't have longer hair on her head like some anthros, but only her natural, brown coat of fur. Some said her eyes were shrewd, though Osien had said, right from the very start of their encounters, that they were "penetrating." Nia had not liked the idea of that at first but she came around to it later. It made her feel as if she saw past what was on the surface, digging deeper and carving out the truth of what mattered

Water did that too, wearing and ebbing away at even the restrictions of rock, letting beauty come through. Nature could not stand up to its own elements, not even then, and Nia had always been so fascinated by the natural world, everything that shifted and changed. One place on the coast would not look the same in the slightest ten years on, yet she still recognised the twist and turn of the landscape from her childhood. It was all interconnected and Nia would not have had it any other way.

She tugged her jacket a little more tightly around herself, the black linen not all that thick – but it was not needed with the warmer air and the lure of summer coming soon. Just the wind could be brisker from time to time, so she was mindful of it. The stoat did not enjoy being chilled and tucked her tail in closer to her body, though her loose trousers were not much protection from it either.

She wouldn't need heavy, warm clothing where she was going, following an old sheep track away from her view of Mawddach estuary. Osien would not be too far, but even the sea serpent could not be around civilisation for too long at any given time, for his discovery, well… There were creatures like him in the world, but one such as him would not be understood.

It was far enough away from the estuary to wear on her legs, muscles aching as she let the quiet of the day wrap around her. The route she took was not popular with tourists and grazed by sheep – though not through every month of the year. The grass was cropped short, but it struggled to grow even with the heavier rains the country usually gleaned, the harsher conditions of the coast challenging at best.

Yet she soon followed the well-trodden path down, her eyes lazily sliding back out over the water as if Nia would catch a glimpse of a hunch of Osien's back out there, amongst the short, choppy waves. The sea was lively that day and there would be few out in it as the wind broke up the swell. It was not the kind of ocean Osien took pleasure in swimming through, the serpent with a long, sinuous body and shorter legs that acted like fins when he was in the water. Still, the serpent could climb out on land too, even if he was comfortable in the salty arms of the ocean he loved so.

The cove offered some seclusion and the caves at the bottom, apparently used by smugglers or those trading goods on the black market some years ago, would keep them away from prying eyes. She hastened along, though her step was sure in her closed-toe shoes, even though they were old and worn, though still with a strong sole. She had never much been one for giving up comfortable paw-wear, even when it was nearing the end of its lifespan.

The wind dropped as she descended to the beach in the small cove, the cliffs seeming to tower high above, though she had seen taller ones. It was how the coast curved around that point that rendered it as secluded as it was and she could imagine ships coming in under the cover of darkness, so heavily laden that they sank low in the water. Yet, once upon a time, that would have been a highly risky endeavour.

I wonder if the reward was worth the price they paid?

Her tail swung lightly and she took off her shoes, curling her bare, exposed toes into the sand. There were shells down there and small pebbles too, worn smooth by the passage of wind and water over them, though the stoat had not come with a bag that day – and neither would she be taking anything home with her. Heart jumping in her chest, as if she was meeting Osien for the first time all over again, she strode to the cave on the left side of the cove, where it dipped into the cliff and the belly of the earth.

"Osien?" She called out, her voice soft and still echoing lightly over the curved, damp walls. "Are you here?"

She blinked, her eyes adjusting to the light. The base of the cave was mostly sand, with some raised rocks on either side, though maybe it had been a channel filled with sand over the years too. There was no way for Nia to understand how it had been, though

Osien, perhaps, could try to paint a mental picture for her.

"Osien?"

"Yes, I am here, dear."

The sea serpent uncoiled himself from the darkness, his blue scales reflecting the light from outside the cave, as if they were set there purely to be a point to draw the eye. His body was long, at least five metres, though that included the length of his tail too. He could have been larger, she was told, but bigger sea serpents tended to grow in the freedom of the ocean while Osien had always stayed close to shore. That was why he'd been spotted over the many years he'd been alive, currently around two-hundred-and-fifty years old.

His head, however, was slim and elegant with a fine, delicate muzzle as he nuzzled into her paws, the stoat inhaling sharply as he curled around her. Even though he walked on four legs, the sea serpent had some snake-like qualities to him, his tail with a large fin to it that had a thinner membrane strung out between the "spokes."

His feet were similar, but with something more akin to webbing between the slender toes. Altogether there was something simply elegant about him, even if he could leave some very strange footprints in the muddied sand of the estuary if he ever came in that close to shore and civilisation again.

"I missed you," he hummed with the music of the sea on his lips, his dark eyes wide, pupils capturing every last little sliver of light they could. "I wish there were easier ways for us to meet."

"I know," she breathed, sliding her fingers over his dragon-like snout, towards the large nostrils that were raised from the top of his muzzle so he could more easily breathe, frills on either side of his face and, of course, one running down his back to guide his movements in the water too. "I know… But I'm looking to move soon. North-East. It'll be quieter there, as long as you are happy to come with me."

He clicked his teeth together, eyes shining.

"Yes, of course," he said. "I think Barmouth may well have had its fill of sea serpents for this lifetime, don't you think?"

She laughed, the sound echoing more obviously in the quiet of the cave. The swell of waves pouring on to the shore caught her attention even then, but the lure of the serpent right there before her was too tempting not to close the distance between them.

She tipped Osien's head up gently to kiss his lips, though his legs were shorter and otherwise kept him lower to the ground. He was not as elegant on land as he was in the water, but his tongue flickered eagerly against her lips, the sea serpent as desperate as she was to rekindle that intimacy and connection between them.

"I missed you," he breathed, though their lips barely parted for the tease of conversation. "So much…"

"You don't have to be without me, not if we go together," the stoat said quickly – too quickly, her words tumbling over one another in their bid to be free of her lips. "I'm so glad you're coming, this is going to change everything between us."

"For the better."

"For the better."

"Always."

She leaned into him as he kissed her passionately. That was something that had taken a little time to work out between her mammalian muzzle and his reptilian one, though Osien didn't use too much tongue anymore.

Osien had not taken too long to learn that, for his tongue was larger and thicker than hers with a tapered tip, always wet with saliva pooling between his teeth. He never realised how much saliva was in his mouth until he slipped from the water to stand on land once more, but he swallowed quickly, keeping it under control. Kissing could be wetter and messier, but Nia had never voiced a single complaint about it.

He groaned into the kiss as it deepened and she moved her tongue against his. They had to tip their heads a little to softly secure the heat of the embrace, lust rising, yet the undercurrent of love thrumming through their connection was all Osien and Nia truly needed.

Nothing would ever break that, but strengthening their bond, again and again, was all either of them wanted. She backed up a little, until the damp rock connected with her back and buttocks, but the sea serpent went right along with her. He moaned into her mouth and Nia's heart leapt and fluttered in her chest, butterflies in her stomach dancing with desire. Her toes curled once again into the damp sand and the stoat was dimly aware she'd dropped her shoes along the way.

"Ah..." She moaned as he broke the kiss, nuzzling down her neck as his large tongue lashed at her fur. "Osien... This... It's been so long!"

Yet her cry was permission as he passionately rose higher, a front foot bracing on the wall beside her shoulder while he grabbed at her top with his teeth. It didn't matter to either stoat or sea serpent that she still had to get home afterwards as he tore both her light jacket and shirt from her body. Osien unduly caught her bra in his teeth at the same time, though neither cared about the heave of her breasts suddenly being freed.

The dragon's lungs heaved for breath, nostrils puckering and flaring, as he nuzzled down her body, dropping heavily back to the sand once more. His head spun with desire and the slit tucked up before his hind legs ached, softening and parting as the head of his member made itself known. It was so quick, a swirl of emotion wrapping around them as a couple to drag them away on the rising tide, but he was there to keep Nia afloat during it.

No… No matter how deep their passion, no harm would ever come to his dear stoat, heart beating strongly in his chest as he yearned to have her. As her clothes hung in tatters from her top half, he nuzzled down hungrily, nostrils catching the flare of salt mixing with her desire.

He couldn't resist, bumping her gently with the tip of his snout as he pulled more gently at her linen trousers. They were looser on her form, but Osien still accidentally popped the button free from its stitching as he tugged them down, though neither minded. They pooled at the sand around her feet and she helped him out by sliding her underwear down, thumbs hooked under the hem to ease them free of her form.

"Osien…"

She breathed his name with true love and warmth ringing through her tone, but Osien did not dare pause. It was too much, the moment strung out between them perfectly as he huffed hotly over her exposed folds tucked up between her thighs. Above him, the stoat's breath hitched and she licked her lips, as if, even then, Nia was goading him on.

A lustful shiver rippled sensually down the length of the sea serpent's body as sand scrunched up between his claws. Even then, his scales were overly sensitive, itching and prickling with sensation. He would have much rather been out in the water with his stoat, but the seas were too choppy to safely take her out that day without drawing attention to themselves.

So, the sea cave with damp walls would have to suffice, salt filling his nostrils as he grunted and lapped out softly against her pussy. The thick, wet slap of his tongue flicked up against her sex and the stoat moaned, backed up to the wall and rocking into his mouth, the two of them as in tune with one another as they'd ever been.

Nia groaned as Osien lapped over her sex, the tip of his tongue teasing into her entrance while it dragged up between her folds, gently parting them even with the gentle pull of his tongue. She shivered, though allowed the sea serpent to do with her as he pleased. They both needed that tangible, clinging intimacy between them, the huffs and pants of snatched breaths, rejoining one another in the very best of ways.

Her tail swung lightly back and forth like the pendulum of an old-fashioned clock, although she was by no means counting seconds at that time. Time had no meaning when it came to being with Osien, her head tipped back and her small, rounded ears brushing back against the rock wall. She never wanted to leave that moment, her hands sliding over his head, thumbs grazing the slick edge of his face fins.

Osien rumbled a growl and lapped up more deeply into her, his broad tongue finding more than enough lubrication to ease past her tight entrance. The moment was right and she heaved for breath, clinging to him and curling her body forward over his head as if she needed some manner of stability right then and there. Osien bore her weight, even as her paws laid more heavily on his head, admirably, though there was most likely very little she could do to push him off-balance in the slightest.

"Mmmph… Yes… Osien…"

She breathed his name, the hard rock at her back standing out in stark contrast to the brush of sea air on her lips. It tickled, easing over where her lips remained damp with a gleam of saliva, yet her chest rose in heaving, needy breaths, his tongue curling up deep inside her. He stretched her entrance easily with it, although there was little the Barmouth sea serpent could do to ready her for his shaft while they didn't have more time and a little more help, though they could imagine. There were other pleasures, other than penetration, for the two of them to enjoy, after all.

"Come with me… Please…"

Osien scooped a clawed front foot behind her buttocks, drawing her out and away from the wall as she stumbled along with him, a shuddering grab at air jolting from her chest. The stoat's tail swung as she tried to maintain her step coming after him, sinking a little more deeply into the damp sand. Nia clung to him, but the sea dragon was in a good position to lay back, slinking his sinuous, almost coiling body down to the sand and twisting so the slit that was parting to reveal his cock pointed upward, at a slight angle.

Nia shrugged off her torn top and jacket, forgetting them in the damp sand. They would not be needed anymore, even if the lack of them would be kind of problematic when she had to go home – but how could Nia even consider that when she was already home when she was with Osien? She squirmed against him as he laid her over his stomach and part of his longer neck, her legs sliding to either side of his serpentine body. It was as if she was riding him, facing down the length of his body towards the rising throb of his tapered shaft, but the stoat's body jolted as the serpent's tongue found her pussy once more.

"Ah – ohhhh!"

She couldn't help but cry out as he lapped over her sex, his tongue dragging lightly up into the crease of her buttocks too. He may not have meant to tease his tongue over her anal ring too, though the added twinge of stimulation drew at her core like nothing else ever did. Her entire body sang with heat as she rocked against him, trying to reach for his cock – but, of course, the sea serpent was too long in his body for her to reach him.

She opened and closed her lips, trying to cry out, though all that emerged from her lips was a breathy, forced sort of grunt. She squeezed her legs around his body, holding fast, yet her body didn't seem in her control anymore, not as she rocked her hips, grinding back on to his snout. Heat threatened to drown her, although she was sure with all her heart that Osien would bring her right back to the surface if ever she thought she was going under.

Osien moaned against her, shuddering at just how close her body was to his, how the stoat laid over his scales as if she could melt into him. Yet there was not a softness to her body at that time, no matter how sensual her breasts felt as they eased over his scales, rocking and humping, even his lungs juddering with the need to gulp air. Of course, Osien could hold his breath for a lot longer than Nia, but it was only natural for him to breathe more evenly when he was out of the water.

His shaft throbbed temptingly, the slick, light pink length desperate for something. However, he focused entirely on his partner, the gritty shifting of the sand around his body barely even catching his attention, tongue disappearing into her sex over and over again. It plunged deep in a lewd, wet slap of the appendage, and he growled passionately against her, the vibrations rippling down the line of his jaw and searing into her.

It was hypnotic, spellbinding, just how she bucked against his face, making his cock twitch and drool, too much pre-cum slopping down the length. That was something Osien had been embarrassed about beforehand, having never experienced sexual pleasure on land before Nia, but the stoat had been quick to reassure him. As sweet as their bond was, deepening the more they spent time together, it was hard to be too concerned about things when a panting stoat was down on her knees with his seed splattered crudely over her muzzle, dripping down her fur.

He shook himself, swallowing hard, though that only brought with it a rush of the stoat's flavour into his mouth. He groaned into her body and lapped up again, mindless in his devotion. It was too easy to slip away, losing himself, though his shaft throbbed with raw need. Sometimes, Osien was sure he could cum without even touching himself at all, but Nia wouldn't allow him to go without, even when he would have focused utterly on her.

His tail flicked back and forth lightly, sweeping through the sand, though his back pressed down into the ground, wriggling and digging a light hollow out of it. Nia shuddered against his muzzle and he pushed his snout even more closely into her body, inhaling deeply as the light scent of her fur flowed through him. Osien so rarely got to smell flowers with salt overwhelming so much and he made a mild mental note to remind Nia just how much he adored the scents she wore. They were small and subtle, but everything came together into a sweeping picture he got to live and relish in every time they were together.

I just want us to be together.

And, soon, they would.

Nia moaned, her body quivering, tail trying to lift – yet she wasn't trying to get something more from him. She just had to ride it out, grunting in the back of her throat, lips moving and still no further sound coming out. His tongue flicked and slurped over her clit and she could hold back the heated rush of need flowing through her for not a second more.

"Ohhhhh!"

She moaned aloud, the sound ripping itself from her dry throat, lips parted, eyes closed. She clung to Osien for some sense of stability, need coursing through her even at the point where it was being relieved. Like waves crashing on the shore, she allowed the storm of climax to roll through her, to take her, his tongue pressed to her clit with as much force as Osien thought she could stand. She could take more than he thought at the point of orgasm, however, even as waves of lust roared through her, bringing her to rises of ecstasy over and over again.

He held her fast, a fin-like front foot up and on top of her to hold Nia on his body. It would not have done to tip her off at that time, but the stoat had never fallen when they'd been in the midst of passion. He heaved and panted, warmer breath rolling over her sex as her arousal marked her folds and dripped seductively.

Nia blinked, seemingly coming too, though Osien was more than ready to curl around her, to find a way to get her clothed again – for he knew it was risky for her to be caught out without clothing. He just hadn't been thinking and a twinge of guilt, that didn't really belong there, pulled at the pit of his stomach. Yet the stoat was too quick for him, sliding from his grasp even as his tongue lapped at the air in her wake, trying to catch her before she reached his overly sensitive, aching member.

She sat up on him, supporting herself with one hand on his scaled body and looking back with a flirty wink and a blown kiss.

"Aw, you know that's not how it works," she chirped, though Nia was still a little breathless. "You've got to relax, sweetheart…"

It was a little easier for her to think after being with him for only a little while, though the stoat would never be embarrassed about the fact she had been so desperate with need for him that they'd barely even spoken before pouncing one another. Still, if it was what they both needed, who could ever say there was anything wrong with that?

No, there was nothing wrong with it, but Nia could not abide Osien being as selfless as he was. They were and always would be equal partners, so she would forever ensure he was as well taken care of as she was.

"Ah… Nia…" He huffed, nostrils flaring. "I…"

But the sea dragon couldn't get out anymore words than that as his voice devolved into a long, needy groan that sounded like it was rolling up from his gut. He twisted under her, his need leaking all over his belly scales, but the sea drake could only hold fast and let the stoat do what she wanted to him. His heart hammered, pounding in the cage of his ribs, fighting to keep his tail from thrashing back and forth through the sand.

"I've got you…"

She swept her paws up either side of his cock, revelling in their closeness, how she could feel every shift and push of his body under hers. The sea serpent couldn't hide anything from her in the slightest and she lapped at the head of his cock, testing just how ready for her he was. With another throbbing pulse of thick pre-cum slicking down his cock, she lapped it up keenly, though even she knew it would not be all that long at all before the serpent lost control.

"Mmm…"

She hummed as she parted her lips around the head of his cock, sliding down. Of course, his cock was far too large for her to take into her mouth easily, but she could still take some of the lightly curved length, the natural lubrication of his member allowing her to get a little deeper. The stoat was not all that comfortable with the tip of his shaft pushing into the back of her throat, so they found other ways to enjoy one another. Her paws were not something Osien had the luxury of himself, rubbing his cock and sweeping up and down in a pumping motion, so she made use of everything at her disposal.

Maybe next time, I can ride him…

She had to take it easy, of course, and work up slowly while taking his shaft inside her to the extent her body stretched around him. That took more time, so their connection that day focused on reigniting their passion, of spending time together in intimacy they could not otherwise share. One day soon, in a more remote home, that would not be such a problem – and they both dearly longed for the days until then to be as short as possible.

He grunted deeply and she chuckled around his cock, bobbing her head at the same time as massaging his length. Yet the sea drake couldn't hold it, not as his cock throbbed and jerked even in the grasp of her paws, her hands just about meeting around the deliciously thick girth. Nia murmured, pre-cum slopping into her mouth as if he was cumming already, yet there was even more to come.

She took her time with him, even if the sea serpent seemed to want to rush to that point of climax and throw himself over the edge. He had not been all that difficult to persuade into letting her please him too, though they would have much to talk about when the deed was done, sitting wrapped up in one another's essence. Nia flicked her tail, tempting him as she sat with her knees wrapped around the sea serpent's body, showing off a view of her rump and the wet folds of her sex.

The sea serpent thrashed and jerked under his lover and Osien shuddered, striving with all his might to be restrained. Yet perhaps the moment was not for such restraint as he thrust up against her, even as the stoat curved lightly around his body to get to his member, where his sinuous form was tipped to the side. No matter the challenges, they found a way to come together, passion coursing through as his length throbbed against her lips.

Osien swallowed his bellow the best he could as the storm rolled through him, need trembling deep within him – but it had to come out one way or another. He rocked against her as his cock jerked, shot after shot of long, hot ropes of cum splattering into her mouth. Of course, the stoat could not swallow every single drop, but she never seemed to care. Pulling back as he twisted and moaned out his delight in his own climax, the stoat let him cum over her, the thick stream of seed pouring down her front. It highlighted the curve of her breasts, spilling over her body, yet there was always more to come with a sea serpent like him, even if it would all wash off easily enough.

A little mess, just like that, was more than okay from time to time, though they might well enjoy time with each other out in the water when they had a more secluded place to be together. She laughed and sat up a little on his body, a paw still on his shaft with her fingers folded around his girth. Letting Osien have everything he needed in every throbbing, pulsing moment, Nia relished in him as much as he lavished attention on her, never letting either one go without.

The spurts tapered off, along with the sea serpent's grunts and groans, managing to stay somewhat quieter than usual as the echoes rang through the cave. Osien quivered bodily and slumped to the sand, twisting gently to lower the stoat to the ground. She easily rolled, sand clinging to her body and the coat of seed drooling down the front of her body, though she still salaciously licked her lips, slurping what she had of his seed down with a truly wicked look on her muzzle.

"Mmm, Osien…"

Nia crawled to his head and cradled it in her lap, neither even considering the mess of semen marking her fur and, with their touch, his scales too. The sea serpent grunted in her lap and tried to lift his head, yet he couldn't quite in the afterglow, ripples of need still resounding through him.

"Soon, we won't have to be apart," she promised, reaffirming what they already knew. "And we will have the life we deserve."

"Mmm…" He murmured, eyes a little glazed over. "I promise."

She chuckled.

"That's for me to promise!"

They giggled together, Osien's tone lower than hers, like their voices were meant to wind together in exactly that manner. Letting themselves sink into the moment, they listened to the waves on the shore, the gulls calling beyond the ocean cave and even the drip of moisture on the walls.

Together, they didn't need anything more than one another, as unconventional as their relationship was.

Under His Boar

"You're where you belong, cariad."

Erin smirked, the boar leaning back on the bed and tensing her abs, while her smaller partner knelt on the carpet between her cloven hooves. Muscle lined her form and bulged through her dark brown fur, though it was coarser and more like hair, darker down the line of her back and lighter, almost caramel-brown in the point across her stomach and down to her lower abdomen.

The bat squeaked lightly, his large ears quivering, though it was all Lewis could do not to let a cheeky grin spread across his lips. He was as naked as Erin was, of course, for there was no need to have clothes in the privacy of her bedroom – and it was, very much, his girlfriend's bedroom. Lewis had kind of expected her room to look something like a bachelor pad when he'd first been invited home with her, but that had been something of a generalisation. Sure, she was a gym buff and big on physical fitness, but there were more notes as to her passions in her room, though she did keep her flat lightly furnished.

The photos on the wall in a collage frame depicted important moments in her life, from the boar graduating with her friends throwing their hats in the air to Erin's more recent trip to Greece, exploring less popular islands. She was not much of a tourist, he'd learned that quickly, but if he was along for the ride in letting her whip him away on adventure after adventure, he'd be in for the ride of his life.

And maybe that was just right for him, the little bat a good two feet shorter than the boar, her muscular body dwarfing his. Maybe it was his size that had rendered him a little less outspoken over the years, though he had other skills, dedicated to painting while Erin had delved into the sciences, though she'd always been drawn to the natural world. They'd met, in the most unlikely at circumstances, at a geology course, where she'd been more interested in the scientific aspects and he the artistry. In a common interest, experienced through varying life experiences, she'd known she wanted him from the first moment she laid eyes on him.

"I know," he murmured, pressing his cheek into her thigh. "What would you have me do, Erin?"

Boars weren't usually as tall as Erin stood at just about seven-feet-tall, but she had a way about her, carving a path before her wherever she went. Of course, that had something to do with her lineage, being a descendent of Twrch Trwyth. Some said they were giant boars, back in ancient times, that wove through myths and legends, chased down by Arthur and his ilk, but Erin had never put much stock in that. It was probably just some other anthros saying that they'd managed to take down a Twrch Trwyth to make themselves seem bigger and better than they were, as was the case with so many in the world.

They didn't need a reason to show up and pretend they were the best, but Erin shrugged it all off whenever comments came her way. She knew who she was and it wasn't any of her business what others thought of her without even getting to know her.

Lewis… Well, he was different. She hadn't ever voiced how the brown-furred bat, with big ears and eyes that were not all that good in terms of sight, got to her, making her heart jump in her chest. Putting a mild arch into her lower back, her chest rose, breasts bare and exposed. The heavy swell of them so very easily drew Lewis' eye and she grinned, her snout wrinkling as she didn't even bother to hide her own amusement with him.

He squeaked and rose up a little higher, his hand on her left thigh. Even then, his fingers could not curl around the boar's thigh in any meaningful way and, sometimes, Erin joked that her thigh was as wide as his waist. It was, most likely, not all that far off.

Lewis took a shuddering breath, the blue hues of the room falling away as he focused on his partner. How was it so easy for him to forget everything, all the stressors of life, when he was with Erin? If he wanted her to laugh, he would have told her it was to do with her ancestry, how the myth thrummed through her, carrying on her line and the lilt of magic in her bloodstream.

But that was not the time as he dared follow the rise and fall of her breasts as she breathed, the bat's eyes roaming lustfully down her body to her midsection and the hint of her oblique muscles. Her abs were not visible at that time, for it would have taken a lot more restrictive of a diet for the boar to lean all the way down – but that had never been Erin's focus.

"Please…" He whimpered, squirming and pressing his knees together, his shaft throbbing lightly as it swelled with desire. "I want you."

"Oh, I know that."

The boar's lips parted, making her pale, white tusks a little more obvious, though most boars not of her kind didn't have tusks that large as sows. Yet she didn't care for how they lightly affected her speech, lending a gruffer, shorter tone to her voice than may otherwise have been present. His eyes flicked up to hers and then back down again. Heat coiled at Erin's core and she parted her thighs a little more to make sure his eyes went straight to the folds of her sex, plump and inviting.

"Mmm, so, show me what you've got, little bat," she teased, yet there was a challenge in her tone. "Maybe I'll make it worth your while."

He wasted no time. There was no question at all in Lewis' mind what the boar wanted from him and he buried his short snout between her legs with a lewd moan that he may have been embarrassed to let loose in other company. Her taste exploded on his tongue as he lapped up inside her, his tongue delving into her sex and her arousal to crudely slurp down all he could.

Ah, but it was not all about Lewis and that was something the bat very much had to remember as he flicked his tongue up between her folds, teasing it up and over her clit. She squeezed her thighs around his head too quickly for him to even consider using his hands, though they may well have helped him out there too. The bat rolled his hips back with a needy whine that he knew would go unanswered – at least until later, when the boar could use him with her appetite whet, just as she pleased.

There was nothing more he loved doing, however, than sinking into the moment. He moaned deeply into her pussy, the musky, spicy scent of her enveloping him. Even then, the earthen tones of her aroma flooded his senses with every snatched breath, heady and desperate.

It was too easy to lose himself there, though the boar would always hold him where he needed to be, both locking the bat in against her and grounding him in the moment. There was no chance Lewis would slip away, no matter how untethered he felt, not with her holding him fast. He shivered, quivers running through his body as if he was trembling in place, but the boar's thighs squeezed so devoutly that it felt like an act of worship simply to eat her out.

He sucked on her clit, focusing on it as her pleasure ruled. Pressing it reverently between his lips, he flickered his tongue over the swollen nub, Erin's need already high, and tempted her to tell him she was too sensitive – which, of course, would never happen. The boar was far too proud for that to happen and, frankly, would only see it as a challenge to hold out through being given oral while over sensitive.

"Mmm, that's right," she grunted, curling her fingers into the bedsheets as she leaned back a little to grind her hips forward into his touch. "Get in there, unff… Good and hard!"

She wasn't put out at all by the bat being rougher with her – what else could she have wanted? Erin, after all, had spent some time already training the bat in the bedroom. Not that they didn't do other things outside the bedroom, of course, but getting to know him more intimately and learning about who he was just made her hungrier for him still, as if she needed to claim him for her own and only her own.

Her tail twitched under her rump and she scooted her hips even closer to the edge of the bed, letting it hang down. It put her in a somewhat precarious position, but she didn't care – wouldn't even have cared if her position sent her slipping off the edge of the bed to the carpet. The bat moaned against her, sending soft vibrations tingling through her crotch, though they were subtle and almost overruled by the pull of his lips around her clit.

She let euphoria take her, the bat doing his best work, her pussy drooling her arousal. Groaning, she licked her lips eagerly and rocked against him, grabbing a handful of the dark brown, nearly black, hair that was tousled atop his head. It was always a mess but she rather liked that the bat kept it long enough for her to grab it, twisting her fingers into it. He shuddered, his wing-arms tucked down with his hands resting helplessly on her calves, scrabbling and trying to find a way up so they could be utilised in her pleasure too.

Her lust mounted, but she was able to control it, squeezing harder to get Lewis to back off without even needing any words at all. Just a little, just so she could better enjoy the ebb and flow of desire and work more moderately towards climax, using him as the bat too relished in delivering the act of service to her.

Lewis trembled, licking around her clit and finding her folds wetter still. Passionately, as if nothing else existed outside the world of her pussy and her thick, muscular thighs, he dove his tongue straight back into her pussy and used the tangy drip of her arousal to add more lubrication to her clit. Attacking it with his tongue, he varied the pressure, swirling his tongue around and using his lips, though it was always the constant, overwhelming assault on her pussy that would get her where she needed to go.

He was not quite the same there, overly sensitive and needing a gentler touch. Even having his shaft buried in the heat of her cunny made him feel like he was going to explode right there and then.

Oh no…

The bat sucked in a breath full of her scent and his head spun, shaft throbbing. He really should not have thought about how it felt to have his cock inside his dominant partner, not when he was so close to her sex. Her arousal dripped down his chin and he groaned into her, his shaft throbbing and aching. He was sure he'd explode the moment his cock even touched her pussy – that was even if the boar allowed him to be with her in that way that night. Sometimes, waiting like that and being "made" to was better than being allowed to orgasm whenever he wanted for himself.

It felt safer like that, handing that control over to someone else who was much better placed to use him as he wanted to be used. At least, it was like that in the bedroom for them, for that was the kind of relationship that best fit the boar and the bat – and that was okay for them. Not that he minded at all if Erin spoke up for him in a restaurant too if a waiter brought him the wrong meal and he didn't want to kick up a fuss.

They fit and he very much hoped to find more ways they came together in such a simple, comfortable fashion in the future of their relationship.

"My bat…" She grunted, squeezing around him. "You're tempted."

Oh, he was, so very much. But he kept himself under control, for he was under Erin's "hoof," her desire the rhythm to which he adored her. As she released her grip ever so slightly on his head, he surged forward against her, sucking hard on her clit as his snout crumpled faintly. He could feel how his flatter nose was being borne back and a thrum of pain warning him that he was being too rough with himself, but Lewis didn't have it in himself to care.

As he slurped into her, the boar panted and heaved and his head ached from trying to look up from between her legs, wanting to drool over her body. However, the boar demanded so much more to him and he wanted to be submissive to her whims, her arousal soaking into the fur on his face, chin dripping with it.

She wasn't in the business of holding back when the moment was precisely right for the climax she wanted and the boar bellowed. The sound echoed off the walls of her room, though Erin had no concern at all about the neighbours hearing her; the one upstairs was as deaf as a post. Not that it was a bad thing to be hard of hearing, but it let her be loud, to let loose with her passions and her partner with all the wild abandon she had in her.

Her hips surged against him and she grabbed a handful of his hair again, more tightly than before, crushing him down between her thighs. He ate her out just as she'd trained him to, though it was, of course, for their mutual benefit. Even to Erin, it was obvious just how he relished in the chance to please her and she wanted to let him take that pleasure too, darting his tongue between her clit and her pussy. Yet it was very much not as if he was unsure of what to do, merely lightly torn between giving her that hard, almost rough pleasure Erin truly craved and getting to drink down the sweet flow of her orgasm.

"Mmmm…"

The boar's bellows softened to a low, deep groan as she rolled her hips towards him, letting the waves of ecstasy thrill her. Her pussy clenched around nothing, her arousal near enough squirting from her, yet it was partly the pressure of his mouth around her sex that gave it that effect too. All Erin needed was to have her lovely little bat right where he belonged, her thighs tensing as she played with him, her head swimming with desire.

It was not enough, however, even as she held him there, asking him without words to keep lapping over her, his tongue determinedly sweeping up around her clit, testing her readiness for more. Erin, however, had other tastes where she could tease her bat and smirked as her gaze went to the certain drawer where some toys were located.

"Fetch the blue one."

He stiffened, ears twitching to catch her words.

"W-what?"

She grinned, releasing her pinching squeeze around his head enough for him to move up. Heat flooded his cheeks and crawled down his neck as he looked down, squirming at the thought of what was to come. He wanted it too, of course, and immediately fished out the strap-on, which was of the type that fit inside the boar's sex with a fat bulb and then had a dildo extending from it at an easy angle for her to take him. The bulb end of it would ease into her while the dildo protruded out from her sex: a popular brand for partners enjoying that manner of shared pleasure.

He shivered, but he couldn't have said he was cold in the slightest, not as prickling heat crawled through him. He licked his lips, shuffling his arms a little as the leathery flaps of his wings than ran down them rustling lightly in a pull of soft skin. The boar stood at the end of the bed when he returned to her, though he had only been a few seconds in rummaging in the drawer for her chosen toy, though she took it off him with a gentle hand.

"And the lube, sweet one."

"Mmm, yes…"

He shook his head again and hid a shy smile, getting the lube at the same time. The blue dildo was gently rounded and tapered at the tip and he had no worry at all about it hurting him, for she would never be too rough with him: dominant, yes, but never rough. It was all exactly as he wanted it to be, though Lewis was finding he could do more than even he had ever thought he could.

Erin pushes me in all the right ways.

"On the bed, my love."

He did as she ordered, though it was said sweetness, with a crinkling warmth in the corners of her eyes. The boar watched intently as the little bat climbed up, the bed a little too tall for him – but she had bought it before they had become partners. Maybe when she replaced it, she would get a slightly shorter one, so he could hop up on to the mattress without having to make a bigger jump. His legs tended to get rather shaky after sex, to be fair…

"And legs up."

The bat sucked in a breath as he did, feeling duly exposed as he raised his legs and held on to them with both hands, just to help himself. Tensing his abs to keep his legs elevated would have worn on him quickly and he wanted to be able to sink into the moment a little more, still in his rightful place under the boar. It was where he belonged and Lewis thought more and more that he didn't want to be anywhere else.

She rumbled a growl befitting a Twrch Trwyth, though boars would not have naturally made such a predatory sound. It was just too tempting when the bat quivered before her, looking up at her with those big, dark eyes of his, shining with desire he perhaps could not yet put into words. She slid the bulb of the strap-on into her pussy, grunting in the back of her throat.

"Mmm… This one is perfect when you've got me as wet as I am now."

He whimpered before her, but he didn't say anything until she uncapped the lube and coated her fingers in it, smearing it around the first two digits of her right hand and spreading them apart lightly. A string of lube pulled between them as she tested it, finding it more than thick enough for her liking.

Lewis squirmed as she leaned over him, keeping eye contact when as her warm hand and cooler lube touched his ass.

"Stay still for me…"

He did as she asked, squirming lightly. It was hard to be still when she was like that, rocking his hips faintly with her finger teasing into his ass. The boar stretched him open gently, though the dildo was not a particularly large one. For them to share in pleasure, it didn't need to be.

Erin took a dollop more lube and smeared it over the dildo too, just for good measure. But there was no need to hold back as she gripped his leg, her strong fingers curling around him, possessively clutching him. With the head of the toy teasing over his pucker, she rolled her hips gently, feeling out his readiness, but the bat, once again, opened up beautifully around her, like he was made to fit the boar in every single way.

The same could have been said vice versa, but she rather liked thinking of it that way around. He moaned under her as she bore down over his legs, pushing his knees back towards his chest, challenging his flexibility and range of motion. The bat cried out sweetly and she murmured to him, easing inside him with subtle rocks of her hips. Each thrust, if it could even be called such, eased the dildo deeper inside, though it would have to reach its deepest point before Erin could feel what she wanted, grinding against the toy for her own greedy pull of pleasure.

She moaned aloud, sharing in his delight as she thrust a little harder, the toy tugging within her pussy. Thankfully, it was large enough that it would not slip out while she was wet, but Erin was more there in the moment to take him, to dominate him, to see her bat coming apart into pieces before her. She'd be there to put him back together again, after his climax left him a moaning mess on the bed, but nothing else mattered in the heat of a moment quite like that.

His shaft throbbed wantonly as she thrust, grinding into him deeply. Something lurched in the pit of the bat's belly and moaned aloud, eyes half-closed – ah, but he had to keep his eyes on the boar, still, for he wanted to see her. He wanted to take in every glorious inch of her as she dominated him, as she took him, every part of the room smelling of her. The boar didn't even have to tempt his shaft by playing her fingertips over it or closing her hand around it in a squeeze and a pump, not when that dildo hit all the right spots inside him.

"Ah… Yes… Thank you…"

"Oh, sweet one," she murmured coarsely. "You don't have anything to thank me for… That'll come later."

Her words sounded like a promise as she speared lustfully into him, keeping the faux cock deep as she ground it over his prostate with every stroke. Not that Erin was specifically trying to, not that time, but she knew what drove him wild, how to gently scoop a hand under his ass to help angle his pelvis so she caught it with every pump. It could have been purely accidental or it could have been a deliberate choice on the part of the boar, licking her lips and grunting as she took him.

Desire mounted in the pit of her belly once more, despite her recent climax. Oh, Erin could have got off time after time again and had her pleasure, but she would have worn her poor bat out completely if she had been so selfish. Even if she was in control, she had to do so respectfully – and that was key to any relationship.

She hungrily eyed up his twitching cock, though he was not as over productive as she may have been called when it came to visceral arousal. Whereas she was soaked between her thighs pretty much as soon as she felt turned on or things got started between them, he took time to be worked up and still did not expel too much pre-cum or semen when it came down to it. It didn't matter, but she enjoyed the comparison all the same.

Her fingers gently brushed it, the hard length protruding straight up and trembling in her grasp. That was the bat under the length, however, his shuddering form sending even his extremities shivering with desire. He moaned the moment her fingers curled around it, but she was gentle with him, coaxing him closer and closer to the edge, about to lose control and spend his seed all over her hand and his abdomen.

"Ah… Erin…"

"Yes, that's right," she groaned. "Say my name, sweet one. Just like that…"

Lewis breathed out her name all over again, trying to roll his hips and arch up against her. Yet his position made it such he was pleasantly pinned under her, feeling the weight of her muscled bulk, her body honed and carved and her mind wickedly sharp too. He blinked, eyelids fluttering as he tried to keep his eyes on her, though not even Lewis could pretend to have control of himself in a moment like that.

It was entirely in the boar's hands, his breath tickling his lips as he breathed between them. His small tail twitched as Erin squeezed his cock, though she didn't even press hard enough to make a heated jolt lunge through his stomach. The lighter tease was more seductive still, her hips pumping to grind the dildo deep, using the pressure of it on her own sex to heighten her own desire.

"Come on, cariad…"

He loved hearing that from her, groaning in the back of his throat, though it was a softer, raspier sound than when a similar sound slipped from her lips. The room suddenly seemed far too warm, as if it was growing smaller around them, his entire world narrowing to his lust with the boar and only her. Nothing else mattered as need pulled with due urgency in the pit of his belly, cock drooling a drop of pre-cum, teetering on the edge.

Erin thrust more urgently, grinding as deep as she could to please herself, the bulb of the toy pushing hard up inside her. Yet the boar had timed things well, allowing the swell of desire to rise inside her at the same time, pushing him over the edge into a broken squall of orgasm. As she ground, his hips pushed hard up against him, coaxing throb after wonderful throb of cum from his length. His balls were smaller, hidden by a thicker fluff of bat-fur, though they'd be there for her to play with if Erin so chose.

The bat groaned, head swimming with pleasure, though Erin held him there in the moment. With his partner above him, pressing his knees finally all the way back to touch his chest, he felt her shudder against him, giving a more savage grind of her hips, pushing against him to greedily savour her own need at the same time.

Yet it was a moment in which they could share, revelling in the intimacy of climaxing almost together, but the bat would need a little while to be ready to go a second time that night. She was more than willing to wait for him, of course, and would have other ways to amuse herself in the meantime while looking after him.

Together, they found ways to make the differences between them work, while investigating the closeness building, bit by bit. It may have only been the early months of their relationship, but there was so much more for both the boar and the bat to learn from one another, and even more for them to uncover.

As the door opened to greater pleasures still, Erin's lips twitched into a half-smile, a hazy, softer look in her eyes.

"You really are something special, Lewis."

His ears twitched, heart soaring, but he was too dazed in the afterglow to respond – yet.

Under his boar, as ever, was simply the very best place to be.

Below the Waterfall

Few dared venture out to the cottage below the waterfall, which was only set far enough back from the falls and the bank of the plunge pool that it would not face too much damage from excess moisture in the air. The land around the waterfall was rich and green, fed by the constant moisture, and there were few times in the year when it felt uncomfortably hot there, even though basking in the sun was a frequent activity around the falls. It was dangerous enough to reside as close as they did, but it was secluded for the couple who lived there: the artist and the biologist.

The Gwiber that inhabited Wales still were feared, though that had something to do with their size. Annest rarely headed down into Abergwyngregyn, the local town, as locals were wary around her. Of course, they had changed over time, finding love and partners in life, becoming more anthro-like over the years, which was how Annest had been born as a naga.

The long coil of her tail settled under her as she perched up on top of it, the naga only dressed on her top half, for she had no need of anything else. However, her soft, flowing blouse still had to have openings for her bat-like wings, which were usually kept folded in against her back and laying against it. It was merely a comfortable position for Annest and not really something the Gwiber thought about.

Annest's dark tongue flickered curiously in and out of her mouth as she sat up at her easel, her brush flowing easily across the canvas on the easel and then dipping once again to her palette of watercolours. It was second nature for her to paint with the ease of motion, knowing exactly where her palette was, along with the glass to clean her brushes. Although her eyesight as an anthro-type naga had improved from what she'd heard of her ancestors, Annest still did not rely on her sense of sight too much. Touch and smell in particular had always been more potent for her, yet her sense of where objects were in the space around her was something she felt she'd developed.

Colours mixed on the canvas as she painted, seeing what she wanted to create in her mind's eye, though it was always such a pleasure to find it appearing on the canvas before her too. She exhaled softly through her nostrils, which flared and puckered gently with her breath, the moment seeming to weave and wrap itself gently around her. It had not always been like that for Annest, but she needed those quiet moments more than ever.

"You always look so beautiful when you're painting."

She started slightly, her snake-like muzzle swinging towards her partner, who was laying along the length of the sofa. Her brush slowed and she smiled with a lightly parted open mouth, the tip of her tail shifting and slithering into her coils.

Her otter partner, Glenna, relaxed against the sofa, propped up on the cushions with a book on crab biology before her. It was not something the otter was personally researching, for their local area, but there had been talk about them going on a research trip to the coast, perhaps even out to Ynys Mon on the northern edge of Wales. It would not be too far for them to go, though Annest could be a little too comfortable in her home surroundings sometimes. If Glenna did not encourage her to go out and experience the world, she likely would have been quite happy with her little routine of looking after her garden, cooking and painting.

It was not a bad life, of course, but there were still more things to life to be enjoyed as Annest had found. The otter was more adventurous, though always took care to keep her boundaries in mind. However, the adder-naga was quite aware that she may well have never met Glenna if she had not gone to a new town one day, curious about some rare books on painting she had heard would be present at a prestigious book fair. To say it had been love at first sight would have been an overstatement (they had fought over the same single copy of a book on painting nature), but it was a part of their story and they adored it.

"Mm, I didn't even know you were watching me," Annest said softly, her coils shifting lightly against one another. "I thought you were reading, darling."

Glenna smiled, the otter brushing her loose, dark brown hair back behind her shoulders. It curled faintly, though she wore it styled naturally more often than not. Wearing much clothing was not all that natural for an otter who preferred to be in the water, but Glenna had on a comfortable, loose pair of shorts that came down to her mid-thigh and a crop top that exposed her slim belly.

In terms of their physical builds, the otter was slimmer than the naga, who held her curves well while still retaining a sensual air to her slithering motions. Even though it was not typical of her species, the naga had breasts too – though they only had the appearance of mammary glands. Maybe the shape of them, lacking nipples, had come about in her ancestry line with the gentle pull of their magic and evolution, but it was not a far leap for anyone to consider that when they had once slithered on the ground without anthro-like body parts at all.

"I was reading," Glenna teased, a glint in the otter's eye as her tail slipped over the edge of the sofa. "But you were altogether more captivating."

"You know you're never going to get me to blush with this snakeskin," Annest countered playfully, pointing her paintbrush at the otter. "It's a failed mission, darling: give it up."

Glenna giggled, rising slowly and fluidly to her hind paws as if the mere motion of standing didn't require any conscious thought on her part. It was strange to Annest how she was always overly aware of where her body was, her coils, at any given moment. She was larger, of course, than Annest and longer too, so she felt like she had to be aware of that, all so she didn't cause any damage to the house.

Of course, a knocked over lamp or two was hardly a bother to Glenna, not as she approached her partner with a sway to her hips that came with the natural ease of her body.

"I don't need to make you blush when I can warm you outside in the sunlight," she said. "I know you could go into the heat room…but won't you come out and breathe some fresh air with me, my sweet?"

The naga glanced at her painting, but she wanted time for a layer to dry before she continued. The scene depicted the waterfall outside their home and mixing colours too much would muddy the edge to the darker background of the rocks and greenery. Only then could she bring out the lighter hues, how the water sparkled when the sunshine struck it just so, capturing a moment in time she wouldn't even have believed was real if not for seeing it with her own eyes. To Annest, it only made sense to show that beauty to others, sharing it as widely as she could.

"Yes…" She smiled, her black tongue flickering and dancing once again between her lips. "I think now is the perfect time for a break with you."

Even though Glenna did not need to, she took the Gwiber's hand and Annest uncoiled herself, slithering along with her to the front door. It was larger and wider to accommodate her frame, tail stretching out behind her with a light S-shape as she slithered. She didn't mind being so close to the ground all the time, though it had made Annest more conscious of where she was going. Roads and pavements, undoubtedly, were the hardest on her body. Homes and being out in nature, undoubtedly, were easiest.

The otter took a deep breath of fresh air, realising she had been inside for quite some time too. She had a habit of getting so wrapped up in whatever she was reading that the rest of the world simply seemed to pass her by, like none of it even existed in the first place. Glenna could fully retreat into her little bubble with her partner in the room with her too, the soft sweep of the naga's brush over the canvas lulling her more sweetly than any music. She had enjoyed listening to relaxing soundtracks beforehand, but there was something about the simple, soft noises of coexisting with someone that were easier on her ear than anything else.

"Ah…" She breathed in again, songbirds flitting through the trees as their tiny, clawed feet clung to slender branches, checking out whether they were a threat or not. "Isn't it good to be outside?"

The naga shivered, even though doing so didn't really benefit her physically: it was merely a habit she'd picked up.

"Mmm, yes… But I need to get warm."

She could have gone into the custom-built room in their house with the overhead lights that both warmed her swiftly (red light) and the ultraviolet lights that gave her the dose from the sun she truly needed. There was much that serpent-types required that mammalian anthros did not, though the Gwiber could be out of sunshine and cooler for longer than many snakes. That was a hint of the magical heritage curling through her still, a spark that would never be extinguished.

The otter smiled, still holding her hand. Her warmth seeped through into Annest and the naga fought the urge to grab Glenna and snuggle into her, using her warmth to heat her own body. It was not such a bad idea…

Yet Glenna knew well enough what Annest needed and pulled her away from the waterfall and the base of the cliff, into the forest. There was a small clearing not all that far away where a couple of trees had been felled in a storm – and the rest of the undergrowth had been gently cleared in the Autumn by them both. It left an easily suitable spot in which to sit in the midst of nature as sunshine splashed down over them.

Of course, there was only sunshine there when the sun was overhead, for the trees were tall enough that they would still cast shadow over the clearing when the sun was further in the East or West. At that time of day, however, only one side of the grassy clearing would be in shadow, giving Annest plenty of room in which to stretch out and sprawl, soaking up the warmth. Other times, she headed to the top of the cliff where there were larger, flatter rocks on top of which to bask on, acquiring more direct heat.

She was not too chilled that day, however, even if her movements at the canvas had been a little slower and more sluggish than usual: enough that Glenna had noticed. With a murmur of contentment, the naga stretched out over the fallen tree, the gnarled roots casting twisted shadows across the grass.

"Mmmm, yes, I need thisss…"

There was a hint of a hiss in her voice and Glenna giggled, joining her by sitting at the end of the log near Annest's head. She pulled the naga's head into her lap and the serpent allowed the otter to do so, eyeing her curiously out of her dark, drawing eyes.

"You should have brought your book," Annest commented. "It's not often you come out here without it."

"Ah, but I have the best company out here with the breeze in the trees, a snake in my lap," she flirted, her tail swinging back against the log, with her hind paws bare. "I need to get you out from time to time, all so you can stretch."

"Hmph."

Annest grumbled and Glenna bit her lip, stifling her giggle.

"I mean," the otter went on. "I need to have you out here to really see how long you are now... You could fit three of me along the length of just your tail!"

Glenna was shorter, to be fair, at under five-feet-tall, but the snake squirmed and wriggled as her head was stroked gently.

"Size doesn't matter, dear," she hissed, her body warming slowly in the splash of sunshine. "But I could wrap around you to keep you in one place and away from your relentless research for a time, if you insist..."

Glenna grinned, no longer even bothering to hide her mischief. Even with the naga's head in her lap, she picked up her hind paws from the grass and kicked them back and forth, the scent of fresh grass and wildflowers tickling at her nose. Annest's arms went up around her waist, holding her gently in the loop of her arms.

"Don't tempt me with a good time."

The naga twitched and looked up at her, twisting around so she was on her back and looking up at the otter from that direction. The tip of her tail wiggled lightly back and forth and the serpent hissed faintly, even the sensation of her black tongue slipping between her lips oddly grounding her. It was funny how those little sensations could be held on to like that, as if they had more meaning in the moment than they did.

"Mm, I could…" Annest considered, a different kind of warmth pooling inside her. "But I'd have to see how a certain otter felt about that. Or maybe she's trying to take advantage of me when I'm just warming up? Oh, it's impossible to tell…"

Glenna, however, had no misconceptions of what she was doing there, even if she could have ever so slightly more power over the naga when she was in need of warming up. That was why there was a big electric blanket on their bed for the majority of the year, although the summer months were a lot easier on Annest. With a small smile, secretive and promising, Glenna ran her hands over Annest's head and neck, sliding her fingers by the corners of her lips and scratching the underside of her jaw.

"Mmmm…"

Annest wriggled, blinking slowly as she watched her partner, that heat within her stirring a little more. Her body trembled inwardly, sending a ripple outward through her, yet her mind seemed to be working more slowly too, as if the cool of the day had chilled her more deeply than she'd recognised. That was okay, however, as the otter slid back, letting her head rest on the rougher bark of the log, scooting herself to the edge so she could pull at the hem of her shorts.

"While you're slow, I could put on a bit of a show…"

Glenna's tail twitched as she eased her shorts down, the snake's chest hitching as her breath pulled. It didn't feel at ease or comfortable there and she longed to be close to the otter as those shorts slid down, baring an expanse of soft, brown fur. She knew for herself just how waterproof that outer layer of fur was, as Glenna maintained it with specific oils for otters, as they swam together whenever able. Annest had been a frequent sight at the outdoor swimming pool before it had closed for winter, though she enjoyed the indoor heated pools more when she found a quiet time to go.

"I like this show," she hissed, her tongue flickering against the side of her snout as she watched the otter pulling her shorts all the way down – but that wasn't all. "I like it all very much…"

Glenna wasn't wearing underwear and she grinned as Annest's tongue flickered in and out more rapidly, tasting the air. The black of the diamond pattern on her snakeskin, running down her back and the length of her tail, caught the sun in a subtle gleam. She knew just how the naga's eyes were between her legs, watching avidly as the soft folds of her pussy were revealed. With her thighs pressing back together, the cup of her sex was mostly hidden from view, a creamier swathe of lighter brown fur teasing down to the point of her sex.

She was far from done, however, as she grasped her crop top and pulled it up slowly, but she would have to do the motion a second time to get the bra off too. Even if she preferred wearing little clothing, the otter still had to often wear a bra just to get the extra support for her chest. Her breasts were on the large side, easily twice as big as Annest's modest pair, but the serpent enjoyed teasing them.

With her crop top off and tossed aside, the otter nipped at her lip. She was fairly sure no one was going to come upon them out there, but she could never quite be sure. Maybe that was what made being flirty and sexy outdoors ever so much more tantalising to her, though not much would top the time she and Annest had enjoyed sex in the lake. Twilight had been falling that time, casting a purple-blue hue over the land, and the water had splashed and splashed as they'd teased and adored one another.

She doubted the naga could hold out for all that much longer without touching her as Glenna unclasped her bra at the back. Her breasts spilled out, freed at last, and the naga's eyes greedily locked on to her, as if it would have been impossible in any way for her to drag her eyes away.

Annest squirmed, that heat twisting through her as if she was the one being wrapped up in the coils of her own tail. Yet she wanted to enjoy the show even as her dark tongue lapped against her lips, slithering a little closer as she rolled on to her front and pushed herself up with both hands.

"You are tempting me..." She hissed, eyes glittering with dark desire. "I need you so much."

Glenna grinned and wriggled a little, backing away with a flirty twist of her hips.

"Why don't you come get me then?"

Annest didn't need to be asked twice, though she spilled the coils of her tail off the log first before striking for her partner. She lunged in the blink of an eye and Glenna squealed with delight, her lover's arms going around her instantly and sweeping her off her feet. In but a moment, Annest had her right where she wanted her: up on the log with her back to the gnarled roots, so she was supported a little more. Of course, the snake didn't waste any time in parting her legs to expose her glistening folds, a tempting drop of wetness marking her petals.

"Ah!"

Glenna only wondered briefly, for a heartbeat of a moment, if she had overplayed her hand, so to speak, but it was all worth it as that dark, sultry tongue flicked up against her in a lewd lap. She cried out and fought the urge to squeeze her thighs around the serpent's snout, wanting more, craving more. Yet how was she supposed to get that when a coil eased around her, lightly holding her in place?

The otter's head swam as the serpent's tongue swept against her folds. The black tongue teased and flickered, dropping a little lower to her entrance. Glenna whined and yelped as the naga licked up inside her, the slippery length of her tongue easing inside as if there really was no resistance down there at all. And, despite the mild size difference between them, there was no question at all about them being equal partners in the relationship. She was only being restricted a little so she could truly enjoy the pull of pleasure as Annest's tongue dragged back against her folds and lapped over her clit.

"Oh… Ohhhh!"

She moaned and Annest smirked against her pussy. Oh, she knew exactly how to tease her partner, though she held out for a little longer herself, waiting for the sun to induce a little more warmth into her scales. She squirmed and lapped up deep inside her partner, the wet slurp of her tongue pulling up and over the otter's clit. Glenna's squeal was all she needed to tease out the otter's pleasure, however, spurring her on to see what other adorable sounds she could coax from Glenna's lips.

Could there honestly be anything more perfect? The serpent's lips twitched into a lopsided half smile on one side once more, though she couldn't bear all that much expression on her face while eating out her partner. Her tongue scooped deep and she took pleasure in dragging it out against the wall of her sex, her tongue teasing over the velvety texture and her slick arousal.

Glenna couldn't help but heave and pant, her breasts rising sharply for every snatch of breath she dragged into her lungs. She needed more, so much more, yet she was at the whim of her partner and couldn't take agency back into her own paws. It was so much better to lean into the moment and let Annest do with her as she willed, for there was a part of Glenna that thought the naga knew her body better than she even knew it herself.

Her hips still rocked, leaning back as far as she felt comfortable. Heat rose at the core of her being, desperate for her and demanding her attention. Just how could Annest raise that point of need in her so swiftly? Yet it was merely as if the rest of the world fell away as she moaned out her lover's name, desire coiling around her.

"Mmmph…"

Yet Glenna did not feel articulate at all in that moment as her hips gave a juddering push and she nipped at the inside her cheek, her body straining to contain itself as it was. Tension pulled at her lower abdomen and she twisted lightly back and forth, though didn't have the heart in the slightest to actually squirm away from the naga. It didn't matter how overstimulated she may or may not have been feeling in the moment, not when she needed Annest even more than she needed to climax.

To get her tongue into the serpent's cloaca-type opening would be reward enough for her, she was sure…

"Ah… Annest…"

She breathed the naga's name as that tongue assaulted her pussy, the otter quivering as it slurped up inside her. It was so thick that the naga didn't even need to use her fingers in the slightest, for Annest was already more than aware Glenna preferred her tongue over penetration with her fingers. Sometimes the tip of her tail would do too, with a slick, easy coat of lube dripping from it so there was less friction as the otter was stretched out around it.

Annest, however, didn't slow her pace in the slightest, though her attack pleasurably focused all the more on the otter's clit. The throbbing nub of flesh felt more engorged than ever as it teased up against the increasingly wet length of naga tongue and Glenna could not help but flinch, ever so mildly, away from its touch.

She needed it too, however, and tried to find a place for her fingers to latch on to around the serpent's head, even if Annest didn't have horns or hair or anything of that ilk to help Glenna out. It was all the otter could do to stay in place, the naga's hands greedily spreading her thighs a little further apart. It was a good thing Glenna was flexible as her leg draped down the side of the log, stretching out without any manner of strain on her body in the slightest.

The strain came in her lower abdomen as lust built and built, her desire not something she wanted to tame in the slightest. With her hips rising and her partner scooping a large yet delicately fingered hand under her buttocks to help lift her, the snake let the tip of her nose rub against the otter's clit. Her tongue lashed inside and Glenna's breath caught, lips opening and closing several times without any sound at all coming out.

The dam inside her trembled – and burst in a splattering of need. The naga's tongue drove desperately back up inside her as she climaxed, her pussy rippling and pulling with no rhyme or rhythm around Annest's forked tongue. Yet Glenna was only present in the moment as much as her orgasm grounded her there, rocking her hips passionately against Annest's snout, needing it all.

Yet she could not stop her messy climax from squirting, painting Annest's snout in her arousal, though the naga's tongue was quick to lap it off, seemingly torn between eating out the otter and savouring her climax. Nothing went to waste, however, as the naga coiled around Glenna slowly, using the twists of her long tail to gently guide both of them down to the forest floor.

For the otter's eyes shone and there was clearly no worry of being caught in the moment in her mind anymore. Annest blinked not so innocently at her. Glenna liked a certain "finisher" after climaxing, after all. Annest may not have understood it for herself, in all honesty, but twisting around so the otter was supported by her tail, resting on the thick muscle of it, with her muzzle close to the parted slit of her cloaca was not something Annest was going to refute in the slightest. Shared pleasure, after all, was the best kind of delight as far as they were both concerned.

"Mmm, you know I wouldn't…let you go without yours too…"

Glenna panted as she spoke, though the otter wrapped her legs around the serpent's tail, delighting in the closeness of their bodies. Her fingers eagerly parted the naga's slit, though her cloaca was not a single entrance to her body but a softer pull of flesh inside. Thankfully for Glenna, the urethra, vagina and anal ring, though a little different, were all separate within there, which allowed her to target her attention more directly with Annest. The slit contained such merely for convenience, though Glenna had a suspicion the naga's innate magic, running through her bloodstream, had something to do with that.

The plush wetness of her inner-cloaca was delightful, however, and the otter buried her face into Annest's scent, moaning against her. Her tongue lapped against the entrance to her pussy, tucked deep inside, and dragged up, seeking the flatter clit and bunching of nerve endings that would make her partner squirm so much she barely managed to stay on top of her tail. Glenna's tail draped sensually down against that very tail as she groaned and lost herself in the moment, her body still glowing with warmth in the afterglow of her own climax.

Yet that would never be the main event for the otter, not when she enjoyed focusing on her partner as much as she did. Annest twisted mildly, not wanting to dislodge Glenna, under the otter and she eagerly curled her thumbs into the naga's slit, helping to part it all the more easily for her delight.

The sunshine had already more than warmed her snakeskin hide but Annest hissed and flicked her tail, shuddering with the restraint it took to not let her coils shift and slither over as much of the clearing as she could reach. No, she had to be restrained, purely to look after her partner, yet she was more than comfortable with where she was in the moment, a ripple running through her as heat spiked within.

She hissed and leaned back, bearing her shoulder blades back into the grass, crushing blades as the scent of fresh greenery tickled at her nostrils. Annest's tongue flickered and slapped against her snout, still tasting her partner so very intimately on her lips and in her mouth. If she could live with that taste forever tugging at her arousal, she would have been more than happy.

It was not quite possible, of course, so she relished in the moment and committed every throb of delight to memory. Even the closeness of her partner rendered her trembling, ripples pushing down the full length of her body, a greater heat still building where the otter's tongue flicked skilfully over her pussy. It teased inside her and flickered back out again in a brush of sensation, building her up slowly and powerfully to a climax the naga knew was going to be mind-breaking.

She was more than happy to rest there, however, feeling adored just as she had devoted so much attention to Glenna. It was up to the otter to bring her to completion exactly as she pleased, though she could not stop herself from quaking as Glenna played her tongue intentionally over all those sensitive nerves that made her blood sing as if she was not cooler-blooded. The magic had a hand in how her body retained and required heat, but she was more than glad it brought the draw of climax to the surface for her. It was not something she would ever give up in any way, not when it brought her as close to Glenna as it did.

It was about far more than the mere proximity of their bodies, but the intimate connection between them, making love out in the forest as sunshine splashed over their bodies. Glenna moaned into her sex again, the subtle vibrations from her lips travelling up deeply into the naga's body, but it was all exactly as Annest wanted it to be.

As need rose within her, she was not in any position at all to deny it or even pretend to hold it off. Tightness roiled through her and she hissed, tongue flickering rapidly in and out of her mouth as she tried to hold herself still, as much as her body wanted to heave and slither. She was right where she needed to be as she groaned and shuddered bodily, the otter's tongue slipping inside her again as she did everything that made Annest's heart sing.

The naga didn't hold back, not as a throbbing rush of ecstasy poured through her. It always seemed to take a while for her to feel it through every muscle and line in her body. Her sex squeezed around the otter's tongue and she twisted as much of her tail up and around Glenna as she could, even though it was a clumsily throw of an otherwise sinuous part of her body. She groaned for breath, arching back and thrusting where her torso met her tail up from the ground, no longer as concerned about tipping Glenna off her tail as she had been before.

The otter would go right along with her as she smirked and lapped into the serpent's sex, her tongue darting with the playfulness of her kind around Annest's entrance, slurping down all her arousal she could. It was thinner and a little waterier from the naga than any other partner Glenna could compare to, but she ran her tongue over the smooth flesh, the contact electric between them.

She was glad the naga twisted around her like that, holding her in place, for she needed the support at that time, an elbow stuck out and her tail flung to the side. Yet she would have put up with any manner of awkwardness in positioning to be with her partner, for they had long ago made the size difference between them work out. Nothing was impossible, much less their compatibility, when they had love on their side.

The naga's body ached with desire, throb after throb coursing through her, though it was everything she needed, riding out wave after wave as if it was a sea serpent's coils she was following the curves of, peaks and troughs allowing her room to breathe as she swam in warming ecstasy. She blinked slowly, trying to come back to herself, yet the tickling tease and sweep of the otter's small yet intense tongue kept her right where she needed to be through it all.

Pressing into her, the otter held on tightly, wanting to be there for every second, every shuddering breath that pulled at her chest. Annest had not bothered removing her top, but Glenna felt she had more than enough to work with, even if she would like to gently slide the top from the naga's form too.

Later, however. After a candlelit dinner and gentle conversation about their interests, listening lovingly and attentively to each other and their various areas of expertise. That faint hint of paint would still linger in the air of the cottage and the naga would lead the way up the stairs, Glenna giggling as Annest took up most of the space and forced her to wiggle her way around her long, flexible tail.

A night together would offer them far more than an interlude in the forest, as pleasant as that was, but everything was there for them both to take, exactly as they pleased.

Below the waterfall, the Gwiber and the otter had so much desire to share in the many years stretching out before them.

The Cat's Whiskers

Cerys peered over the harbour wall from the side where the cars would park, her long, black tail swishing back and forth wickedly. It was hard for the cat anthro to hide at the best of times, at her size, but that didn't stop Cerys. The harbour slowly filled back up with boats returning after the morning of fishing or checking lobster pots off the coast, but they would spend the rest of the day stocking their catch to be sold right off the harbour. Some restaurant owners would come down to get the freshest fish, while others would go to the local fishmonger, who was always in high demand.

Her mouth watered, her vest-top tugging under her arms as she tried to remain as discreet as possible, yet Cerys often drew attention at an easy six-foot-three. She was more powerfully built too, with broader shoulders and wider hips, as if everything about the feline was made to be eye-catching, her shoulders rounded out nicely with muscle and her biceps defined even through her black fur.

"Any minute now…"

Her pale whiskers twitched as she watched one fisherfur, an old, grizzled canine with flat, floppy ears and wrinkles around his sagging muzzle, going through his catch. The dog anthro had already gone through much of it and was down to the last couple of grates, needing to sort through for any fish that would not make the cut for sales. Those would be thrown back into the water for the waiting gulls and, sometimes, a couple of seals that followed the fishing boats back in, hoping for those very scraps. Animals were canny like that, hunting down an easy meal.

That was one reason why Cerys was drawn to the harbour, tucked in below the town on the cliffs above, again and again. The fishy aromas in the air could be off-putting to others, but she rather enjoyed it, the scents brisk and sharp on the fresh, sea air.

Gulls called out overhead as they swooped and dived, seeking out scraps of fish, though there were certainly some fisherfurs who were forced to jealousy guard their catch for fear of opportunistic seagulls. They were more often than not more of a problem for tourists, purchasing laverbread and cockles from small stores, but there'd been cases of customers of the bakery, Y Popty, having fresh loaves, still warm from the oven, being snatched out of their paws.

Cerys was more the sort to attempt wheedling a good deal out of the fisherfurs selling their catch, but she'd much rather play a trick some days. The feline grinned too widely as the old dog pulled out his final crate, which should have been full of fish.

Only, it was not. The dog with brown ears and dark eyes started, dropping the crate and spilling a slew of pink, blue and white fish over the floor. They were the gummy kind that stuck to one's teeth when they were eating and Cerys' fur fluffed up in anticipation as he threw his paws in the air.

"Who's gone and done this?" He shouted, though he didn't manage to get much volume on his gruff tone, despite the booming tenor of it. "Cough up now, where's me catch? You'll pay for this! What kind of trick do you think this is?"

On, and on, though Cerys laughed aloud for the sheer joy of it. The fish gummies were good – even if they might well have smelled a little on the fishy side after coming out of the crate, which only made them even better in Cerys' opinion. The cat grinned, unable to hide her toothy, white grin, her tail flicking back and forth.

And then the old dog, Ol' Gruff, looked up at her, his eyes meeting hers where Cerys had pushed up over the wall, only set up a little higher than the dog who had been out on the sea since the very early hours of that morning. He scowled darkly and raised his fist at her, but they both knew he wouldn't catch her if he chased her.

"You! It's that cat again!"

Cerys bristled, standing up taller and putting her elbows on the wall, despite the rough stone digging into her fur and flesh.

"Hey, I've got a name, you know!"

"What've you done to my catch? You'll pay for that!"

The cat scoffed, puffing out her cheeks and rolling her eyes.

"If you used your eyes to look, Gruff, you'd find them on the other side of the boat," she chirped, unable to keep up any kind of bad mood for all that long. "You can keep the gummies though – it was worth it to see you stomp around like that!"

The dog growled and made as if to storm towards her, but he wasn't going to catch the town trickster. Well, it was not as if Cerys got in the way of many, even if she could have done so, but it was far too entertaining to see the reactions of the older furs, the ones who didn't have too much of a sense of humour but didn't really kick much of a fuss up over her either. She told herself she was keeping things interesting for them, keeping them on their toes, but the elderly ladies in their knitting club tended to dote on her more. It was a fight every time she visited to chat with them, however, not to bat away their balls of wool, like an innate instinct that made her want to purr and play and *chase*.

Cerys leapt up on top of the wall in one fluid motion, her loose trousers cropped at her calves. She dressed simply, though her hind paws were left bare that day. It just felt more natural for the black cat.

"Catch me if you can, Ol' Gruff!"

Then she was off, spinning on her heel and leaping away, running over the top of the wall as her hind paws moulded to the shape of the old, lichen-marked stone under them. She grunted with the exertion, heart pounding, yet her air of feline grace did not yet fail her.

As the fisherfurs laughed behind her, good-naturedly, of course, she charged up the cliff-side path for pedestrians: too narrow for vehicles to traverse. That road was an easier one to follow and hers was steeper, though Cerys' stamina would not be challenged. She sprang lithely up the mostly smooth path, a couple of steps not bothering her at all in rougher sections, feeling the muscles of her legs bunch and extend, powering her forward.

Soon enough, she was at the top of the cliff again and looking back down into the harbour and the ocean, her tail flicking and curling through the air. The cat's whiskers quivered as the wind ruffled through her fur, though she grimaced and stalked off with a casual swing in her hips.

"Hm. Will need a shower again, after this…"

Cerys loved being by the ocean, but salt crystals clinging to her fur, thrown up in the misting spray of water on the rocks, left her feeling stiff and unclean. She fought the urge to wash off instantly, for she had to reach her home first, but her cottage was not all that far.

She liked to be close to the sea, at a point where she could look out and see more of her surroundings. Which was why her cottage was set close to the edge of the cliff with a road between the front of her garden and the edge, the ocean glittering and stretching out before her. With the sun glancing off it, it would be hard to claim the notion that the ocean was not alive, though the sunshine warmed her dark fur and she shivered pleasantly. She'd lay off swimming in it, but staring dreamily out at it and watching the lives of other anthros pass by from her little bench would always be one of her favourite past-times.

Her small garden was full of brightly coloured flowers at the height of summer, though the sea on the Welsh coast kept her nice and cool most of the time. Cerys was not much of a gardener, preferring an eclectic approach to wildflower sowing around the borders of her garden with a grassy area for sprawling, but she liked watching the insects come to the plants. The rocky wall that surrounded her property was home to all manner of bugs too, which gave her endless hours of entertainment when she was home. Her job in the local museum kept her casually employed without overwhelming her and, of course, it was another place in which she could meet plenty of new furs too.

"Hey!"

Wyn greeted her by poking his head out the front door, the white deer standing with a smile on his face. Cerys' heart skipped a beat at the sight of him, though the stag was a good bit shorter than her. Whereas she was over six-feet-tall, he barely came up to five-foot-four, making them quite the odd couple around town.

"Hey, darling!"

She purred, sweeping the smaller stag into her arms, his antlers a little smaller than they usually were. Wyn's eyes were a perfect blue and she dipped him in her arms, sweeping him backwards down low to the ground as Cerys kissed him passionately. The deer grunted against her lips in surprise, although Wyn was more than used to his larger girlfriend's antics and quivered against her, practically melting into her touch.

"Mmm!" He gasped, the kiss breaking as Cerys grinned and pulled him back upright, setting him comfortably back on his cloven hooves again. "You've got to stop surprising me like that!"

"Oh, but I know how much you love it," she purred, reaching out to stroke his cheek and trail her fingertips up to his antlers. "Are these new? They look fantastic on you, sweetheart."

Wyn blushed, the transgender stag nodding.

"They don't look too obvious?" He asked, turning his head from side to side so Cerys could get a good look at them where they sat behind his ears. "I've been growing my hair out to hide them."

Whereas the feline anthro didn't have hair like some anthros, just her fur, Wyn had a white fluff of hair between his ears. It grew in short and ruffled and would have spilled down the back of his neck if he'd grown it longer, but he was much happier keeping it like that.

"Hm…"

She observed him carefully, peering closely. It would never do to not give an honest opinion, as the stag did so enjoy having a nice set of antlers on.

"They look good," she said with a tone of voice that could not be argued with, as if there could be no other possible answer. "They sit nicely and the bases are well-hidden by your hair now. The clips coming around the back of your ears blend very nicely with your fur. Turn your head for me?"

The stag obligingly did so, moving his head a little more swiftly to see if the antlers moved. She nodded approvingly.

"Perfect! Though they would always be such, especially when they're on you. Personally, I loved those blue ones you tried before."

Wyn chuckled, leaning into her and resting his head on the cat's shoulder as her arms, naturally, went around him.

"Thank you," Wyn said, his voice a little lower and shyer, as if he would never quite lose that vulnerability around his partner. "I like to blend in though and these match."

She smiled and took his paws, drawing the deer gently inside while the door drew closed behind them with a solid "thunk."

"I know and you should always look as you feel the most comfortable," she said. "But you don't have to blend in to make anyone else feel more comfortable."

"I know." Wyn chuckled, shooting her a look. "But I'm still not buying those custom-order antler wraps that had tiny fish on them, not even for you."

"Awww, but they were cute!"

She laughed and pulled him back into the house they shared, with the old stone floor in the kitchen and entranceway, though she had updated some parts throughout. The home still had the old, white-washed walls and exposed beams, which gave the cottage a cosy feel. It could be a little small for some, but she didn't need to keep too many possessions around. They did, however, have a second wardrobe in the spare bedroom, along with Wyn's gaming set-up, for the deer enjoyed a variety in clothing and even Cerys needed some more formal wear from time to time.

For Wyn, she'd wear whatever the little stag wanted, her heart leaping in her chest as a smile stretched her lips.

"Mmm... It feels like I haven't seen you in forever, darling..." She purred, pulling him through to the base of the narrow staircase. "Why don't you and I slip upstairs for a bit?"

"What? You've barely even been gone a few hours!" Wyn quipped back at her, though his lips could not help but break into a smile. "Cerys… Where have you been?"

"Ah, I can't tell you that," she chuckled. "That would be giving the game away, dear. Come with me…"

Wyn laughed, though his large, petal-shaped ears lifted curiously, tail twitching. He went readily with her, his cloven hooves clopping more loudly against the stairs as they ascended than the cat's. Of course, Cerys merely walked backwards up the stairs. Her feline grace had her folding her hind paws up on to each step as if she knew exactly the height and incline of each one, even though they were not even in the older cottage. She had walked them so many times before, yet her sense of depth and her perception of her surroundings was unparalleled.

Maybe it was just Cerys. Maybe it was the black, towering felines she was descended from, one of those creatures that had become something a little more normal in Wales. The descendants of Cath Palug, and many more powerful creatures of the country, evolved and found peace over time, becoming a normal part of the world.

Well, Cerys hadn't *told* anyone apart from Wyn that she was one of the Cath Palug, though not quite as tall or ferocious as her ancestors in the old tales. They just felt that "otherness" about her, the fact that something was ever so slightly different. Sure, the feline had her job in the museum and she'd lived in Wales her whole life, with her family known in another small town away from the ocean, but she'd never fully eased into a community.

But she had more than enough of a place there with Wyn and her friends, Cerys' co-workers at the museum. It was all she had ever wanted and she grinned as she drew the smaller deer into the bedroom with her. It was their own, but often piled in thick blankets on top of the duvet and sheets in winter, for she felt the chill easily. Her fur fluffed up in the winter months, but Cerys' summer coat was thinner and silkier, with a glossy, rich shine to it. Wyn may have been drowned in blankets from time to time, but keeping Cerys cosy was something he was keener on than his own comfort. He could fit in anywhere, but he didn't have to as Cerys looked after him.

"You didn't tell me where you were this morning," he pressed, even as Cerys rolled him lightly on to his back on the bed, neatly putting the stag under her like she'd done it a thousand times over. "You weren't up to trouble again, were you?"

"Oh, like you could do anything about it if I was..."

She purred, lightly pinning his arms back on either side of his head, though Wyn would be pleased to know that his antlers did not move in the slightest, even as his head bumped back on to the thinner duvet. They were definitely a good pair and she'd have to take a few photos with him later, getting shots from every angle so Wyn could see what else of his they would match with. As they were pale, however, they would likely match with most clothes he generally looked good in, but Cerys was always up for a little fashion show and adoration of her partner.

Not right then, however. She had far more of the deer to adore, her tongue rasping out against Wyn's neck as she playfully held him down, easily overpowering the deer with her larger body. He squirmed against her and whimpered, but that only goaded her on, her black tail sweeping back and forth. To anyone observing her tail, they might have thought she was stalking her prey, but Cerys was merely revelling in her conquest.

As she would, every single day, for the rest of their lives together. Wyn squirmed and rocked his hips up against her, but she had a knee between his legs and he couldn't really bend his legs enough to dig his hooves firmly into the bed. That meant he couldn't thrust up, for Cerys blocked his way, but Wyn wouldn't have had it any other way.

Their lovemaking was gentle as their lips met, but Wyn would forever enjoy being on the bottom under her. It just felt right, even if they had not yet dug deeper into why that was, why the control and power felt so much better-suited in Cerys' paws rather than his own hands. Maybe that was something they could explore in future years together, or even months, for their long, comforting summer together stretched out with few plans until the Autumn.

Wyn moaned into her mouth, his head awash in thoughts of the cat holding him down, maybe even having his wrists bound. He'd grown more confident lately, initiating sex where he had been too shy to before, speaking up more in public when he would have preferred before to hang on the sidelines. He'd even made more friends. So, maybe there was more room still for growth and he allowed himself to relish in a soft feeling of submission, imaging Cerys' body pressing even more heavily down on him, pinning him with her physical body.

"Mmm…"

Cerys withdrew quietly as she kissed his face, lips caressing the side of his muzzle and then down his neck. Her teeth caught at the skin beneath his pale fur and her need rose.

"Mm, I need you," she purred, following her wants without shame, as she always did. "Let me taste you…"

The deer half sat up as Cerys pulled back up on to her knees. Even in such a position, the cat seemed to tower, her tail flicking back and forth, though even that could not draw his eye. He was too focused on her body as she drew the vest top up over her head, exposing her breasts. Wyn hummed softly, enjoying the show, though something still tickled in the back of his mind.

It was hard to think of it, however, as he stared at her body longingly, his gaze raking over her large breasts, which near enough spilled out of her bra. It was well-fitting for her, but with breasts as large and as full as hers were, there was little that could be done to keep them under wraps. Even when Cerys was clothed, they drew the eye with the swell they made through her clothing, but Wyn would not have been so rude as to stare when they were out in public together.

In private… Well, she could enjoy him with her eyes and her body as much as she wanted and vice versa too, of course. Wyn squirmed as her paws went behind her back, unclasping her own bra with fluid grace and flexibility to free her breasts.

Oh, wow…

The stag would never tire of the spill of her breasts falling free from her bra as she slipped it off her shoulders and tossed it aside. Wyn would have to dig it up later, from wherever it had fallen in the bedroom, but that was by the by as he raised his torso a little and grasped at his own shirt. The jeans and T-shirt were casual enough for hanging around the house, but it would not be for much longer that he'd feel comfortable in heavier clothes. The warmth of the summer begged a lighter manner of clothing and he needed to find his shorts so he could feel the breeze on his legs again.

He wouldn't get the chance to take his jeans off by himself, he was sure – not as Cerys scooted back to the bottom of the bed and, somehow, sinuously unfolded her legs off the edge. Standing on the carpeted floor, she stripped off her light, cropped trousers without ceremony, even though the flick of her tail pulled at them, making it a little more difficult. Wyn's eyes locked on to her breasts as they hung with the shift in the angle of her torso, the cat bending forward to tug the trousers off her hind paws.

"You look amazing…"

She grinned, hooking her thumbs into her Brazilian-cut panties and pulling them down while she was there, not wanting to wait any longer. Her moderately muscular body was left on show, her thighs thick and powerful while her glutes rounded out nicely. Although Cerys liked to visit the gym a couple of times a week, she built most of her muscle and fitness from her usual activities, though she had taken up rock climbing of late too. A cat like her would always be active, even if she rather enjoyed an afternoon nap in the sun too.

Naked, the cat licked her lips and looked over her partner as if Wyn was a treat to be devoured, though she could have spent hours kissing and caressing every inch of his body. Even then, a part of Cerys ached to lap over the subtle scars on his chest, though they blended in nicely with his fur, as they'd remained paler on him. Still, she knew they itched from time to time, even if they were merely a mark of how far Wyn had come in his life, though she would not have gone as far to say his transition. That implied he "needed" to reach something, an arbitrary goal other furs had placed upon him, when that absolutely was not so. As long as the deer was happy, he didn't have to conform to any "stage" or appearance of transition and she made sure to let Wyn know that every day.

And she'd get him more of the special cream that soothed the surgery scars too on his narrow, lightly muscled chest. In that moment, she pounced on him, unwilling to let there be more space between them, not when she could be pressed up against him, whimpering and wanting. Yet Cerys was not the kind of feline not to get what she wanted, kissing him all over his muzzle and letting her hips roll down against him.

The stag's arms went around her, hands on her backside squeezing, and she trembled under his touch. Even after so much time together, Cerys marvelled at how his touch on her body felt like she was being shocked with a warming electric thrill each and every time, her back arching deeply into his touch. There was something about being with Wyn that made every time feel like the first time, despite their time together. Only, it got better and better every single time.

Yet the Cath Palug was not about to be denied her stag and she licked her lips as she fought with his jeans. Fiddling with the button, she pulled it free and slid the zip down, the sound making her ears prick. It was funny how the little things like that could be so poignant, but they flitted into the background no more than a moment later. She purred as she undressed him, wanting to see him in all his glory, exactly as he was.

Wyn's breath caught in his chest, giving a small shudder, as he was revealed. His jeans were pulled down and Cerys purred, drawing them gently off his hooves and then going for his underwear. The loose, comfortable boxers were perhaps the easiest piece of clothing to remove, although Cerys still eyed the rise of his hips as he pushed them up from the bed, making her task even easier.

"Mmm, I can't wait to taste you…"

She murmured under her breath as she unveiled the deer's sex, tucked up between his legs. His folds glistened with a hint of arousal and she rumbled appreciatively as she couldn't resist taking up her rightful space between them. Wyn didn't have a chance to ask what she was doing before she was kissing up his inner thighs and lapping over his sex, gently parting the deer's folds with the flat, flexible length of her tongue.

"Ah!"

Wyn squirmed, though he couldn't help rocking his hips up against Cerys' tongue, wanting more even then. His hands fluttered, not quite knowing where to land, but they found their place on her head, fingers curling behind her ears. He scratched lightly, though even that tiny motion was not enough to distract him from the blissful assault of her tongue. Pleasure arced through him and, still, his body tried to squirm faintly away from it before he had adjusted. But that would come soon and he moaned aloud with delight, lips trying to curve up at the corners in an almost goofy, open-mouthed smile.

"Mmm, let go for me, honey…"

She purred against his sex and lapped up deeply inside the deer's cunny, her skilful tongue easily parting his folds and devouring his essence. The sweetness on her tongue pushed her on and she dragged her tongue sensually up against his clit, teasing the bud of flesh – but not too much. As fun as it could be to lock her lips around it and suck until Wyn twisted and bucked in unbridled pleasure.

No… She had to be patient, working her partner up slowly as he grunted and chuffed. His voice was lower than it had been when she'd first met him and she loved being along with Wyn for his journey. He groaned, licking his lips, and she peered up from between his thighs, letting her tongue play sensually between his clit and his entrance, stimulating the sensitive nerves and letting his body warm to her touch.

He was amazing, beautiful in the moment, the rise and fall of his chest, his antlers digging lightly back into the pillow and still staying in place. She splayed her paw out flat on his upper thigh and across the point of his hip, holding him still where she could give him all he needed. His sweetness on her tongue begged more and she growled passionately into his sex as her tail lashed and her tongue swept against him.

The deer moaned and tried to rock his hips from side to side, though it was so very much better to give in to the pleasure and that twinge of over sensitivity. Once he was past that, the heady swell of heat inside him heaved and rolled, forcing a breathy pant from his lips that felt like it was driving the air out of his chest. Yet he could still gasp another grab of air, his fingers curling around the base of the feline's ears, easily losing himself in the moment.

"Mm, ah… Cerys…" He breathed her name in reverence, almost amused by how her name sounded coming from his lips as his pleasure mounted. "Yes… Please…"

"I've got you, darling, I've got you."

So, she did, letting the stag ride her tongue as she allowed him to move a little, rocking with the shift of his hips. Her tongue delved greedily deep, scooping up his sweet yet tart flavour so she could savour it all the more, though they were there in the moment together, lust and love carrying them onward.

Wyn moaned and clutched at her, though she slowed the pace a little. Her own body burned for attention and her tail flicked, barely able to contain herself. There were times where she was more forceful with her partner, called on by his grunts and groans, sitting on Wyn's face while the stag ate her out to a yowling climax.

She wanted to dote on him right then and there, however, teasing his clit by circling her tongue around it, not quite touching. A couple of fingers spread his folds apart so she could easily access every part of him, groaning in the back of her throat while her tail gave a needy flick and sensual, feline ripple.

Wyn moaned and shivered, his tail twitching where it was pinned between his backside and the bed. Yet the stag had no will at all to move as heat prickled through him, wanting to dig his cloven hooves down into the bed so he could buck up against her. He wanted more, craved more, yet his lips parted, wishing he had his sweet cat's pussy buried against his muzzle, wanting her above all else.

"Mm, ah… Cerys?" He drew her attention, though it took a few, chuffing breaths before he was able to raise his voice loudly enough for her to catch it. "Please… I'm so close, but…I want to taste you too."

She raised her head, propping her chin up on his thigh, tail lashing the air. Her green eyes practically glittered in the afternoon light of the bedroom, the curtain drawn halfway across so they were not in direct sunlight. Not that either of them would have minded at all baring their fur like that, feeling its warmth sink into them.

"Mm, of course…"

She moaned lightly as she shifted positions, following the lead of Wyn's eyes as if they were moving together in perfect synchronisation. The feline let his touch on her shoulder encourage her to roll over on to her back, though Cerys sprawled far more dramatically across the bed, the sheets rumpling faintly under her back. She stretched her arms out over her head as Wyn's eyes went to her breasts, watching how they rose and fell with her exaggerated motion.

"Hm…" He hummed, shaking himself so he didn't fall prey to his own need instantly. "So… What were you doing down by the harbour? I'll not start until you tell me."

She mewled as he teased her verbally, pouting a little. But she wasn't trying to hide anything.

"Hmph, well, I was playing with Arthur again," she admitted with a wicked, flashing grin. "Ol' Gruff, he loves that nickname. You know all those fish gummies I bought? He didn't like having his catch swapped out for them!"

She giggled and snorted, tears in the corners of her eyes. Yet the stag could not resist laughing along with her, his lips tugging up as he chortled, trying not to lose the moment. But what could be better than sex, truly, than sharing it with someone like that who could make them laugh?

"I can't believe you keep aggravating him," Wyn chuckled, eyeing her up as his attention returned to what he really wanted. "Cerys…"

"Oh, don't *Cerys* me like that!"

She grumbled and slid down the bed a little, her head flat on the mattress rather than propped up on a pillow. But the stag licked his lips in a way that gave her pause, sucking in a breath that halted her words, if only for a moment.

"You know I'll always be there for you, Cath Palug," Wyn teased, crawling over the bed towards her as the stag's head dipped subtly, inclining his antlers. "But I can't always get you out of trouble, if you're out at the harbour swapping fish for candies."

Cerys giggled, but there was a wicked glint in her green eyes.

"Oh, I can't make any promises…"

But they had one another to focus on, the lustful rise of their need demanding attention as their heartbeats beat in time with one another. Or closely enough that they felt in tune with each other, like they were one and the same, Wyn crawling over her and kneeling astride her head, facing back down the length of her body. The stag tucked his chin down, looking back at her breasts, but let out a squawk that didn't sound very deer-like at all as she grabbed his hips and pulled him to her lips.

"Ah! Cerys…" He moaned, shuddering as his tail flipped up, revealing the white, fluffy underside. "Ahh… I can't reach you…"

With their slight height difference, pleasing each other at the same time could be a little more difficult. Cerys, however, had feline flexibility on her side and released her grip on the stag enough for him to fumble his way down and nuzzle against the front side of her pussy, a breath above her folds and the swollen bud of her clit. It would have taken less of a height difference between them, however, for him to push all the way down between her legs to lap into her sex, but it hardly even featured in their minds at all.

It was Cerys who sat up, curling her torso forward and easily tensing her abs to keep the position, not bothered in the slightest by the strain it put on her body. She was primed and ready, her pussy gleaming with her arousal, but it would not take long for Wyn to explode in bleating bliss.

Her tongue lapped into him, though she trembled as he kissed her clit, playing his tongue across it as his hand took care of her entrance. She was soaked already, so Wyn had no trouble at all in sliding first one digit and then a second into her pussy, grinding his fingers deep and a little rough, exactly the way she liked it. Moaning into the deer's sex, Cerys' fur dampened with his arousal, though she wasn't about to let up that time until she felt him bucking passionately against her face.

She knew exactly how to bring him there, but the eager stag's desire was not to be set aside so easily. And he was intent on slurping around her clit, not being anywhere near as gentle with her as she was with him, putting more pressure on her bud as he sucked *hard*.

Wyn grunted against her, ears twitching, his body aching with the need for climax. His blood felt hot, rushing and coursing through him, but he couldn't slow his pace, not as he worked his fingers quickly into the tight, squeezing wetness of Cerys' pussy. Her sex hugged his fingers, gripping and pulling as if she wanted them even deeper, but the stag could get her right where she needed to be. That was not something Wyn had any concern about in the slightest, rolling his hips as his pleasure mounted and her arousal dripped on to his fingers.

Yet, in the end, he couldn't hold back as the feline flicked the tip of her tongue rapidly against his clit. It was too much, the subsequent sucking pressure making him groan aloud and gasp, lips parted as orgasm heaved through him. She closed her lips passionately around his clit, as if he was the only thing in the world that, like there was no one else who could ever come close, the stag grinding on her face.

He didn't pause, however, not as he squeezed a third finger, though it was a little more difficult, into her pussy. Warm swells of pleasure billowed through him, his sex closing and squeezing, arousal soaking her muzzle, but he couldn't stop, wouldn't stop, not with the cat's scent infiltrating his system. Wyn couldn't help but inhale as deeply as he could, sucking in the breath with snatched glee, the faint scent of her natural fur and her musky arousal pulling at his senses.

He groaned and let his fingers curl up inside her, doing his best to draw the pads of his fingers through her sensitive passage, her sex twitching around him. It was not direct enough to stimulate her G-spot, although his fingers still pleasured the sensitive nerve endings inside her, the feline letting out a raspy hiss between his thighs.

However, the deer was right where he needed to be as he grabbed at her thigh. Even though Wyn was on top, it still felt like he was in a submissive position, at least to him, the cat well and truly leading the way. He pressed his lips harder around her clit, wondering if he would need to pull the edge of his teeth over it too – although the cat was already there.

The Cath Palug moaned and grabbed at him, struggling not to collapse back on to the bed as orgasm wracked her to her core. Her whiskers quivered, relishing in the taste of him on her lips, how his sweetness soaked into her fur. Yet she needed it all, even more, hungrier for Wyn than she had ever been. One round, at least for her, would never be enough when it came to lusting and loving her partner, yet she revelled in the thrum of energy pouring through her, pussy squeezing around his fingers.

Together, they let orgasm take them, though Wyn was coming down from his while the cat got to enjoy hers, dosing his fingers in her arousal, strung out luxuriously between his fingers. Cerys' chest heaved as she curled up against the stag, her legs still spread for him, though the rolling, throbbing pulses of climax sent flowing, glowing heat through her in the soothing afterglow.

Slowly, she slumped back to the bed with a pant and a shuddering gasp, chest rising sharply with a needed lungful of air. The stag slid down on top of her, but Wyn still had enough presence of mind to wriggle around so he was at least laying facing in the same direction as her. The feline drew him to her, so he could rest his head on her breasts, a low, rumbling purr rising from deep within the feline's chest.

"Mmm… I needed that."

She smiled as he rested, both of them recovering, at least for a little while. Her tail twitched faintly, although Cerys was already looking forward to the next round, where she could dote on Wyn and lavish attention on him even more. She was sure there were still some nice, cooling massage oils in the cupboard that the stag would absolutely adore being used on him.

"I needed it…you…too…"

Wyn mumbled under his breath, eyelids heavy in the aftermath, though it was easy to lean into her and the moment as her paw crept down to his hip again. A small touch like that felt like electric zapping into him, shivering in turn.

They could take as much time as they wanted with each other, for there was never any rush. But Wyn was more than ready to keep his frisky "little" feline occupied, even if it would not keep her out of mischief.

Together, they'd found their place in the world and wouldn't be anywhere else.

Birds of a Feather

"My singing voice is all tapped out today," the blackbird said as she flopped on to the bed, her black feathers gleaming after her shower and powder, all to keep them in pristine condition. "Oof…"

Although Anwen was exhausted after their singing, she stretched out, her arms heavily feathered to give them the appearance of full wings. She had hands at the tips of them, of course, but the songbird couldn't fly, which she would rather have liked to do. The only one of their trio who could fly was Glain, the hippogriff with dark wings extending from her shoulder blades, rather than having wing-arms just like her.

And then there was Siriol, entering the room with a flutter of feathers, the gryphoness bearing a similar type of anthro body to Glain. Anwen was the only one with wing-arms, although Siriol had not been blessed with the ability to fully lift her body from the ground. Her black wings were smaller and more delicate, not allowing her the grace of flight either.

What rendered all three avian anthros similar, however, was their blackbird ancestry – though, of course, what else could possibly be expected from the Birds of Rhiannon? Gryphons and hippogriffs traditionally came with more predatory avian features, although other species were not unheard of too.

Anwen's beak was narrow, a light yellow-orange that was fine and delicate. Like most avians, her eyes were set a little more to the sides of her head, giving her a mild blind spot in front of her, although it had never bothered the blackbird. Her feathers were a traditional jet black befitting a blackbird, although her legs and talons, where her feathers came to an end with softer, smaller feathers on her upper legs, were a darker shade still that looked more orange most of the time.

Glain had an easy smile about her, though it showed more in her slightly more forward-facing eyes than any expression that could come through in her beak. Even though it was clear she had blackbird heritage about her torso, wings tucked in against her back as she sat on the bed next to Anwen, her beak was thicker and shorter. It was far from the beak of a bird of prey, but there was something a little more daring about it that those who saw her usually couldn't quite put their finger on.

The equine half of the hippogriff's lower body, however, was a rich, deep grey with dapples splashed across her rump. Her tail spilled down from her buttocks in a black waterfall, always well-groomed and looked after – but avians tended to be particularly finicky about self-grooming. Naked as she was, Anwen chirped at the sight of her, letting her gaze roam down her partner's form, though the blackbird was not the only one who could lay any kind of claim to the hippogriff.

Siriol the gryphon, on the other wing, was darker in colour still with smaller wings than Glain, though her beak was chunkier still with a more predatory shape to her head. One might have thought twice about whether she was a carnivore or an omnivore, though the tiny tufts of black feathers at the points where her ears were hidden gave her a more gryphon-like look about her.

Still, it was blackbird in her ancestry, even if she had shaped herself to her personality over the many years. Her tongue flicked softly against the edge of her beak, which had a downward curve at the tip as if it was just about to round into the more distinctly formed beak of a bird of prey. Her black feathers, as ever, were sleek and glossy, while her lower body was that of a large feline – perhaps a leopard or similar. However, she bore the dark colouration of a black panther, as the reference to the melanistic colour variant of a leopard went, so many mistook her hybrid species there.

She didn't care. It took a lot for the gryphon to care about anything, which was one more reason for Anwen and Glain to be grateful for her joining them all that time ago. The Birds of Rhiannon had been together for so long, they barely even knew what they would do without each other, but their voices had lifted the status of the singing trio so many new furs around Wales, England and even Scotland knew of them. Soon, they would start into Ireland too, visiting both the North and South for a tour that would hopefully spread the sweetness of their song further still.

"Do you ever find it strange," Glain commented, running her fingers over the silken feathers on the top of the blackbird anthro's head as she trilled. "Strange…that we sing to entertain now?"

"What? Instead of sending anthros to their eternal sleep or raising them from an everlasting slumber?"

Of course, it was Siriol that quipped that, lightly rolling her forward-facing eyes. Glain chuckled, feathers fluffing up in amusement, but they were swiftly smoothed down once again.

"We could still do that," Anwen mused, as if the blackbird was really considering it. "But…where would that leave us?"

"Mm, the world is different now," Glain agreed. "It was an interesting time though. A lot more shift in the hierarchy of the country."

"And that was only in Wales," Siriol scoffed. "With everything in the world as it is now, don't you think we can do some good?"

Anwen parted her beak in a smile, the lightness of it showing in her eyes as she shuffled up on to the pillows, opening her arms for Siriol.

"We will spread softness with our songs still, Siriol," she said gently, even as the coarser type of gryphon grunted and allowed herself to be bundled up into one of her partner's arms. "Calling those back from the brink, or those who have only just passed through the veil."

"Sometimes it doesn't feel like enough," Siriol murmured, the gryphon seeming to deflate. "We are so different... Fitting into this new world is not something I ever anticipated needing to do. At least... At least I fit with you."

Glain trilled and cuddled up behind the gryphon, though the hippogriff still hugged her wings in close to her back, keeping them out of the way. At their size, they could be a little overt – and certainly required her to have clothes tailored for her with how they needed to slip through cut-outs in the back.

All three of them together worked well, though they had their squabbles still. They were only birds, after all, even if their songs had greater powers still. But the world would soon tell if the dead began walking again, as the ability to do such a thing had long ago been relegated to the world of myth and legend.

They should have been such too – and yet they'd lingered, they'd grown. There were little nuances of the old times like that still filtering through the land of Cymru and likely beyond too. But Adar Rhiannon did not concern themselves with such things, not when they had their own affairs to manage. Still, others like them were around, even if the avians kept themselves mostly to themselves.

Siriol clicked the edges of her beak together and nuzzled into the light rise of Anwen's breasts. Even though birds did not usually require them, her form had naturally shifted to such over the years. The gryphon and hippogriff, on the other wing, had always had breasts complete with small nipples, with Siriol's being larger and heavier, accentuating her curvaceous figure. That was their mammalian hybrid sides showing through, but they had found the magic flowing through their veins amenable to a little shift in their forms, even if it took several years to evolve, in a way, through them.

Siriol took a shuddering breath and nuzzled her beak into Anwen's neck, trailing the tip down to the point of her shoulder. The gryphon flicked her black, leonine tail, the proximity of their bodies rendering the moment gentle and warm. In their bedroom, the curtains were cast open to allow the early evening twilight sky in, the first stars appearing splashed across the visage there, but there were still a few puffy clouds in the sky.

Their bedroom was large enough for all three of them, the bed bigger than what many would have had in their rooms, but it had to fit all of them comfortably. Glain in particular liked to stretch out, though her dark wings ended up fanned out over the top of the other two more often than not. Her equine tail flicked as she ran her clawed, bird-like hands down Siriol's front, teasing over her breasts and then, very lightly, dragging the rounded edge of her claws around the gryphon's nipples.

"Mmm…"

Siriol shivered, yet the moment was perfectly right for all three of them as Glain nipped teasingly against the back of the gryphon's neck, pressing up even more determinedly against her back. All three of them were naked, but that wasn't what aroused them, the thrill of singing on stage in yet another show still glowing through them.

Anwen tipped the gryphon's head up and kissed her neck with little, pecking kisses, easing down her neck. Siriol shivered and rocked against her, though the gryphon appeared a little torn, not knowing truly whether to push back or grind forward. Each option was equally desirable to her and she flicked her tongue up against the outside edge of her beak.

"Ah… You two…"

"Just relax, Siriol," Glain cooed. "Let us take care of you. I know how you stress before a show, but you are always fantastic. You deserve every last one of their eyes on you, all on you."

"Ah… They're looking at you too."

As much as Siriol tried to praise the others, it was hard to say anything with the others teasing her like that. The gryphon's claws played tantalisingly over her nipples and she squirmed, trying to squeeze her thighs together.

Anwen was far too swift for her to keep up something like that for long as she kiss-pecked her way down the gryphon's body to her stomach, lingering there for a moment in sweet adoration. Yet the blackbird was swifter to ease between Siriol's thighs and raised the right one, leaving her laying further rolled over on to her left leg. As if they were all flying perfectly in sync with each other, they all knew where the other was, how to move together, but their lives were blended in such a way it seemed simply natural.

The hippogriff grinned and nipped playfully at the back of Siriol's neck, pressing in close to her. Yet she was there to support her partner in the moment as her other partner slipped two fingers over the gryphon's soft folds. They were small, yet the gleam of moisture as they parted betrayed her arousal, Siriol's need rising even then. The blackbird's beak teased gently between them, pulling up over her clit, though she would use everything she had at her disposal to hear her partner sing.

Glain let her hips roll against the gryphon, languishing in the moment. Her shoulders ached somewhat, along with her upper back, from taking to the air for a section of their show, though it never was a surprise to her just how much effort it took to fly. There were few anthros who could do it, after all, though she had enjoyed a fling with a dragoness in her younger years, before the birds, who'd had the most spectacular wings.

She sank into the moment, however, a part of her revelling in how the gryphon trembled against her. Siriol was wonderful, so brash and coarse on outward appearances, although she had a softer side to her, as if all that show and bravado was just to cover up something. They'd all faced their trials over the years, with family and friends and the shift of the world around them, but none of that mattered when they slipped away to their own reality.

Anwen, however, took her job seriously of teasing the gryphon, playing her tongue skilfully around the gryphon's clit, which easily swelled from within the tiny tuck of its hood. Siriol squirmed against her partners, gasping aloud, though Anwen wasted no time in teasing a single finger into the gryphoness' hot, tight pussy.

"Mmm, you feel as wonderful as always, darling…"

Anwen murmured her adoration of the gryphon with true warmth calling through her tone. She needed it, so very much, her tongue dipping ever so slightly lower to taste Siriol's essence. It was light, so very sweet, and fed a hunger in her for more, wanting the gryphoness even as she vowed to make her keen in pleasure.

Her gryphoness was so sweet, even if she pretended otherwise. Gently, she eased a second finger into Siriol's pussy, stretching open her sex around them, though she could take quite large toys, for them, when they brought them out of the "fun drawer" to play. Under the gryphoness' body, the sheets rumpled and twisted, Glain at least helping out by supporting Siriol's raised leg, so she didn't have to tense her muscles too much in trying to keep it up in the air. Her tongue traced the edge of the gryphon's folds, though she had to still press her beak in quite closely, considering that her tongue didn't really extend out past the limit of it.

Glain squeezed her lover's breasts, fingers digging lightly into the soft flesh. Her tail flicked, though the hippogriff was more than happy with her role there in that moment, desire coursing through. Soon enough, she'd have what she needed from all of them, but it was always the intimacy and closeness she wanted, knowing that all three of them were in it together. The bond barely flickered between the times they were able to best feed their relationship and connection, forever returning to find it as strong as ever.

Siriol's head spun and she moaned, rocking her hips against Anwen, although the push of the hippogriff against her back at least helped her stand firm in the moment. Her chest heaved into Glain's grasp, yet she was more than happy to be fondled like that, the hippogriff's hands easing over her nipples as tiny ripples of electric delight ached through her. She grunted, working her beak and trying to release the tension in the pit of her stomach, yet that would only come with the throb of orgasm. She had to hold out, to allow her partners to do with her as they willed, for they only ever had her best intentions at heart.

She could trust that, exhaling as breath flickered over the nares in her beak, taking the place of what would otherwise have been mammalian nostrils. Siriol tried to squirm, putting more weight on Glain's hand where she supported her leg, but those fingers pushed deeper inside her, working their way back and forth, bringing a flushed rise of pleasure to the gryphon's cheeks. Thankfully, the feathers on her face hid the heat from view, Siriol grinding her hips, trying to push down on those tantalising digits.

Just how did Anwen know how to hit all the right spots inside her? Even when the blackbird had called her on to the bed with her emotions in a flutter, wings shuffling against her back and just unsettled.

Anwen groaned, adjusting her position as she flicked her tongue over the gryphon's clit, though she could just about lap if she tried – it just wasn't natural for a bird to move their tongue like that. But things changed as the years passed and she had a little more flexibility in her tongue, like the gryphon and hippogriff too. She pressed on, heart pounding in her chest, need coursing through her form. It was just as alluring to Anwen to bring one of her partners to the brink, the gryphon thrusting more urgently against her tongue, begging for that touch more pressure that would send her over the edge.

And the blackbird was more than ready to give it to her, working two digits back and forth with a curve to the tips of her fingers that helped her tease up inside the gryphoness' slick passage. Siriol's heat clung to her, hand drenched in the gryphon's arousal, but she was not about to slow down or pause in the slightest as she brought her partner to the edge, the hippogriff nipping and nuzzling at her neck, teasing past and under the feathers to sensitive, pebbling skin.

Siriol's head spun and she shuddered between them, caught up exactly where she needed to be. She groaned and parted her beak, but the others didn't capture it in a kiss, not that time. The hippogriff playfully pecked at her and she quivered, only slightly embarrassed by how sweetly and softly she crumbled before them both. It was not the kind of pleasure she wanted to hold back from, yearning to throw herself into freefall, lustful waves coursing through her.

Tension built at her core, heat spilling over, and the gryphoness did not stay the storm of orgasm for a single moment longer, not as a shrill cry cut through the air. She twisted and rocked through climax, the other two needing to grab at her thighs and hips to hold her in place, though they would have moved right along with her too if needed. It was all about being flexible and going with the flow of the moment – and the birds had never been all that rigid in their approach to life, it had to be said.

Anwen warmed with shared pleasure as her partner climaxed on her fingers, a sweet flow of arousal dripping from her pussy. The gryphon's sex clenched and clung to her fingers, rippling erratically around them, but she was right where she needed to be as she helped Siriol ride out every throbbing, keening moment of her high. It was for her, all for her, and the blackbird would not see the gryphoness relinquished until she was panting on the bed.

Glain nipped at the gryphon's neck as she pecked, as if she was using her beak as a muzzle with teeth rather than the beak she had. It was so worth it to hear her partner moan just like that and she only wished she could exchange a cheeky, yet flirtatious, look with Anwen too. The blackbird surely was ready for more, even as they kissed and pleased and clung to Siriol through her climax.

Siriol blinked, the pulsing waves of ecstasy softening a little, easing down inside her as a warm glow spread to take its place. She exhaled, the gryphoness far more settled than she had been what only felt like minutes ago, but that was the beauty of having partners that knew her as intimately as they did. Keening more softly, her voice barely raised above a breath, she shifted her weight to her back, her partners helping her lay down comfortably.

"Mm, I'll be ready…in just…a minute…"

"Oh, dear," Glain giggled, the hippogriff leaning over her with a smirk, her breasts hanging below her chest as she rocked on to all fours. "I think we've worn you out… But you rest up, we'll be ready for you again exactly when you are."

"Is that so?"

Anwen pulled up from between the gryphon's legs and gently cleaned off her beak, though the blackbird wouldn't have minded a little mess lingering there for longer. Yet she longed to be back in the arms of Glain, the fire flickering at her loins needing the hippogriff's touch.

They pressed together alongside Siriol as she rested, nuzzling and chirping against one another as they laid their beaks together. Of course, they could not kiss like mammalian or even reptilian anthros with beaks like that, but they could peck and "kiss" in that manner, but there was only one thing their wandering hands had in mind. Anwen grunted faintly as she was pushed with need on to her back, the hippogriff sitting astride her head and facing back down the length of the blackbird's body.

"I've got you…"

Anwen would have had something to say in response to that, but she couldn't get a word out as the equine lower half of the hippogriff perched over her beak. She would have sat more heavily if she could have been certain of where the blackbird's beak was, but it was the longest of their beaks and it was still something to be careful of, even then. The blackbird tipped her head at a slight angle, her arm coming around the front of Glain's thigh and pussy so she could play with her clit too, pressing the small pads of her fingers over it.

The hippogriff jerked above her and she ran the very tip of her tongue around the entrance of her pussy, teasing the sensitive nerve endings there. She didn't need to press her fingers deep, of course, to get a reaction, Glain already panting and moaning on top of her.

"Ah… Yes…"

Oh, how she loved the blackbird eating out her pussy, teasing her and making her see stars. Glain's eyes wandered to the gryphoness still sprawled out on the bed, though she looked a little brighter and perkier, more interested in what her partners were doing. She'd join in when she was ready.

Yet the hippogriff was far from idle as her body rippled with flickering rises of pleasure, leaning far down over the blackbird's form and kissing the mound of soft feathers above her pussy. Her gently pecking beak teased between her legs, perfectly positioned to gently rub the curve of her beak over the avian's clit. Her tongue flicked out lightly, curling and sweeping over and around the nub of flesh, readily rendering it slick as her saliva added a touch of lubrication.

Anwen's leg twitched under her and the hippogriff smirked privately. As warmth soared through her, warming her all the way to her extremities, Glain pressed on, her tail flicking above Anwen's head as she worked two fingers easily into the blackbird's pussy. Her sex clung to those fingers, hugging them tightly, and she once again appreciated just how wonderfully the avian moulded to her touch.

It was the perfect moment, rendered even more so as Siriol joined in again and crawled to them, swapping her attention between hippogriff and blackbird to enjoy time with them both. She teased her beak around Anwen's breasts, nuzzling into them, though there were no nipples there for the gryphoness to focus on. The blackbird's flesh was more than sensitive enough, however, to have her quivering under her, Anwen moaning lustfully up into the hippogriff's pussy.

The gryphoness kissed Glain's breasts where they hung beautifully before her chest, tipped forward over the blackbird. Her nipples were more sensitive as she caught them, very lightly, with the tip of her beak and tugged, making the hippogriff grunt and shoot her a look, even though she was otherwise engaged.

The moment, however, was for all three of them at once, now that Siriol felt like she was more awake and settled in herself. She kissed down Anwen's body, her tongue flicking out past her beak with a little more reach than that of the others, both her and the hippogriff "battling" playfully for precedence over Anwen's clit. The blackbird's grunts and groans were all she needed, panting lightly, even her warm breath adding to the stimulation around Anwen's soft nub, lightly pulsing with blood flow and warm where slick arousal tried to cool on her sensitive flesh.

The blackbird, however, couldn't hold back when there was so much going on there, all at once. She rocked her hips and, even then, slightly tried to twist – but it was not as if she wanted to buck or jostle either of them off her. Grunting into the hippogriff's pussy, she doubled down on her efforts, even if she was not quite in a good position to use her fingers to penetrate Glain, utilising her fingers and the tip of her beak, as gently as she could, to bring tingling pleasure to her entrance. Her fingers pressed down with greater force, spreading out a little, over her clit, so they could push back and forth, rubbing and helping the hippogriff with a particular kind of grinding motion she so loved.

Every one of them was different, after all, all preferring different types of stimulation when it came down to it. But it was merely a mark of how well they knew one another that they could vary how they approached even something as common as oral sex between them, applying different techniques to each partner. Anwen didn't want to hold it as she trilled and climaxed, each throbbing swell of pleasure pouring through her with such a pulse and a "grabbing" sort of demand to it that she lost sense of her surroundings.

The blackbird's trill twisted into something of a chirp, like the sound she really wanted to let loose was stuck in her throat. She clung to the hippogriff, holding on tightly, fingers digging into Glain's thigh. The hand on her pussy stuttered for but a moment, distracted by the coursing flow of her own orgasm, though she had more than enough focus to know she wanted to bring the hippogriff to a shrieking high too.

Glain could have laughed as the blackbird doubled down on her efforts, but she should have anticipated Siriol joining her in it, the gryphon running her hands over her breasts. Siriol felt the weight of them, allowing them to spill into her hands, and flicked her thumbs over the hippogriff's nipples as Glain ground on to Anwen's fingers with resounding passion.

She couldn't hold back and neither did she want to hold back, not as desire spiked inside her. It flared up, thick and fast, searing through her like wildfire, but the hippogriff chased it down fervently, ready for it. When it crashed over her, both of her partners guiding her there, she rounded her shoulders and shrieked, the cry slashing through the air.

The blackbird pressed on, easing her beak all the way up to the hippogriff's pussy, letting Glain's arousal drip into her beak, so she could taste her sweetness. It was as potent as an aphrodisiac to her and she nudged in even closer with a groan. There really was nowhere else she'd rather be, her hips grinding back as pleasure washed through her, Siriol's beak suddenly on her neck, nipping and pulling.

"We've got you this time, Glain," Siriol chirped, the gryphoness smiling with an open beak as she reached between her thighs, stroking through her own wetness. "Heavens, I love when you moan like that..."

Together, they all slumped to the bed in one another's arms, limbs tangled, fits of tired giggles shaking their bodies. Yet they were all right where they needed to be, thoughts already turning to a spot of food to sustain them and perhaps a couple of drinks to ease the last remnants of tension from the show from them. After that, they could return to bed once more and show one another, all over again, just how far they'd come together, what they meant to each other.

The Birds of Rhiannon found their way in life and their place in the world, but they never would have done so without each other.

Translations & further information

Welsh to English
Cymraeg i Saesneg

Abergwyngregyn – A village on the edge of the Carneddau mountain range

Adar Rhiannon – The Birds of Rhiannon

Afanc – Monster

Cariad – Love, term of endearment

Castell – Castle

Castell Gwys – Wiston Castle

Cath Palug – A monstrous cat associated with Arthurian mythology

Ceffyl dŵr – Water horse, from Welsh mythology, a creature similar to the Scottish kelpie

Cymraeg – Welsh

Cymru – Wales

Cynwyd – A small village in Denbighshire

Draig coch – Red dragon

Dryslwyn – A castle above the Tywi Valley

Dydw i ddim yn siarad Cymraeg – I don't speak Welsh

Gwiber – A giant serpent in Welsh mythology, often depicted with wings

Lloegr – England

Llundain – London

Shwmae – Hi / hello (informal)

Sut wyt ti? – How are you? (informal)

Twrch Trwyth – from Welsh mythology and the Mabinogion, a wild boar pursued by King Arthur

Y Gwyllgi – A canine-type apparition said to appear in Wales

Thank you for reading and I hope that everything was very much enjoyed!

Ready for more? Check out my author website for more furry fiction and where you can purchase my books!

https://linktr.ee/amethystmare

Cover art by Alena Bodrova.

Gabe Maxfield has reached a comfortable point in his life. His past troubles in Seattle are all but forgotten, he co-owns his own business, Paradise Investigations, with his best friend Grace Park, and he's happy in his relationship with sexy cop—his neighbor—Maka Kekoa. Maybe the best part is, no one's pointed a gun at him in weeks.

Knowing his luck, that is bound to change. Lack of clients and money forces Paradise Investigations to take a job helping Edwin Biers search for a treasure he promises will be worth their while. Gabe has a knack for finding trouble, though, and find it, he does.

A NineStar Press Publication

Published by NineStar Press
P.O. Box 91792,
Albuquerque, New Mexico, 871099 USA.
www.ninestarpress.com

Title

ISBN: 978-1-947904-17-0

Printed in the USA
First Edition
November, 2017

Also available in eBook

ISBN: 978-1-947904-16-3

Warning: This book contains sexually explicit content, which may only be suitable for mature readers.